She Calls Me Daddy

Zoey Zane

Copyright © 2023 Zoey Zane

ALL RIGHTS RESERVED. zoeyzane.net

No part of this publication may be reproduced, stored in any retrieval system, or transmitted, in any form or by any means, electronic, mechanical, photocopying, recording or otherwise, without the prior written permission of the author/publisher, except in the case of brief quotations within the context of reviews.

This is a work of fiction. Names, characters, places, and incidents either are the product of the author's imagination or are used fictitiously. Any resemblance to actual persons, living or dead, events, or locales is entirely coincidental.

Cover Design by Jillian Liota – Blue Moon Creative Studio
Author Logo Design by Tanya Baikie – More Than Words Graphic Design
Editing by Rachelle Anne Wright – R. A. Wright Editing
Proofreading by Dee – Dee's Notes Editing

Dedication

To the friendships that surpass our differences and disappointments.

Epigraph

You can take your "I'm okay" hat off now.
It's just me.
Fall apart. I'm not going anywhere.

— Erin Van Vuren

Fair Warning

She Calls Me Daddy is a companion story to *He Calls Me Bug*. If you haven't read that one yet, please do so for the best reading experience. All characters in this story are of legal age. There are instances of abuse (physical, psychological, and sexual) and cheating, none of which are between the two main characters, Sky and David. If any of these triggers make you uncomfortable, this may not be the book for you.

Prologue

David

PRESENT DAY...

Screams fill the space in the next room. Not the good kind, either—the kind that make you drop everything and run. When I enter the living room, Bug's doubled over in pain and clutching her waist, tears filling her eyes.

"Bug?"

The moment she looks up at me, I know what she thinks before she says it. "Hospital. Now." She steps toward me but loses her balance. "Oh, shit!"

I reach out and catch her before she hits the ground. "I've got you." We walk over to the couch, and I help her sit down. Spinning around, I scan the room for my shoes and keys.

My heart breaks when I return to the couch and her eyes meet mine. I crouch down and cradle her head in my hands. "Oh, Bug." I kiss her forehead before scooping her up in my arms. She's never felt more fragile than she does right now.

We reach the car, and I fling the back door open. "Watch your head." I tuck her into the back seat so she has more room. "It's okay, Sky."

Her face scrunches as she struggles to take a breath. Sweat lines her upper lip, smearing her lipstick. I kiss her forehead again and gently squeeze her arm in reassurance before I close the door and hop into the driver's side.

Hooooonk!

The sound of the loud horn startles me. It's not the first time I've hit the horn in the past five minutes, but I swear to God, if people don't get out of my way, they'll need a hospital too. My blinking hazards, high speed, running red lights, and blowing through stop signs are more than enough of a warning for an emergency. Waiting for an ambulance would've taken too long; however, a police escort would be lovely.

I turn left at the light and slam on the brakes as a semi pulls into my lane and nearly slams into me. I growl and hit the steering wheel in frustration. "Get the fuck out of my way!" I yell at the driver.

"He can't hear you." Her small voice sounds off behind me—not her usual self. I whip my head around.

"Lie down. We're almost there."

A tiny smile flutters across her face. "You're not the boss of me."

Fuck. Even in distress, the twinkle in her eyes doesn't disappear. "Skylar."

She immediately lies back down in the seat. All I have to do is say her full name and she's a pile of wet mess. Sadly, this time it's not for fun.

I will not let anything happen to her. Ever.

Still, I can't help the smile that appears on my face. She's in tremendous pain and somehow still manages to push my buttons.

She's made perfectly for me.

That's why this hurts so much.

Oh, shit. Yep, that was a police car.

A glance at the speedometer tells me he probably clocked me going sixty-five miles per hour in a forty-five zone. With my hazards blinking, hopefully I won't get pulled over.

Not three seconds go by before the police car pulls out of the parking lot and turns on its lights. Usually,

I would slow down and pull over, but not today. I push the gas pedal down a little harder, and before he catches up to me, the hospital's emergency room is to my left.

I pull in and slam on the brakes, honking the horn three times before getting out. "Someone, help!" I yell, and run around to the other side of the car to open the door for Bug.

"So dramatic," she sighs, rolling her eyes. A wave of panic washes over her as she sees a nurse with a wheelchair running toward us.

"Just breathe. I'll be right there." I help her leave the car and say to the nurse over my shoulder, "My girlfriend, please help her."

The nurse nods and helps Bug into the chair. I close the car door, but before I can turn to help, I see the police car turn into the bay and flip the siren on for a second to get my attention.

"Excuse me, sir." His car door barely opens before he calls for me.

Taking a deep breath and letting it out slowly, I turn around to face him. "Yes, Officer?"

"Is everything okay here? You were going mighty fast back there."

"My girlfriend, she's—" I shake my head, unable to finish my statement.

He takes out his small notebook and writes something down. "Go park your car and meet me inside at registration. I'll be writing you a warning."

"Thank you, Officer." I nod and get back into my car. It's all I can do not to scream. That's not exactly the police escort I wanted. I drive to the parking lot and pull into a spot. Before I head into the hospital, I take a few moments to breathe. I've had speeding tickets before. It's not the warning I'm worried about—it's Bug.

The officer is waiting for me at registration and starts to speak when I approach. "Get your girlfriend checked in, then let's talk. They've taken her back already for an evaluation."

The same nurse from outside walks out of the triage room holding Bug's purse and hands it to me, along with a clipboard. "Please fill out the information as best as you can, including insurance, and we'll take you on back."

I nod and reach for a pen from the cup on the desk. Filling out this form is tedious, especially knowing what awaits me. I wring my fingers through my hair, clenching my jaw. Once everything is completed, I scribble my signature on the last page and hand the clipboard back to the nurse.

"Thank you, sir." She types something into the computer. "It looks like they've admitted her to room 201 in the east wing. You'll go through these doors"—she points to the right—"then take the elevator to the second floor and make a right. Walk to the end of the hallway, make another right, and you'll see the nurse's station for check-in." She hands me a name tag.

"Okay, thank you." I take my visitor's name tag, peel it off, and stick it to my shirt.

The officer walks toward me with a long, thick notebook. "I know you're in a rush, so I'll make this quick. I don't know where you were coming from, but if you need to go sixty-five in a forty-five, call an ambulance next time. The citizens of Crimson will thank you. License, please."

It's still in my hand from registering Bug in. I hand it to the officer, then glance around the waiting room while he writes down my information. A moment later, he rips off the top piece of paper, hands me the pink copy with my license, and then adds the white and green copies to the storage compartment at the back.

"This is a warning only because you ended up here. Next time, you might not be so lucky." He looks at me with a softened face. "I hope everything is okay back there. And please, slow down next time."

"Yes, will do. Thank you, Officer"—I pause to glance at his name tag—"Burkley."

"Have a good day." He tips his hat to the nurse at the desk and walks out.

I groan and walk toward the elevator, praying Bug is okay.

I reach the second floor and briskly walk to the nurses' station at the end of the hall. "Skylar Wyatt's room, please." The nurse points to her left, and I take off before she can say anything.

What I see next stops me dead in my tracks.

Chapter One

David

Twenty-four years earlier...

You haven't seen a perfect sunset until you've seen it set over the Coronado Bridge. The different hues of blue and lights connecting the bridge to the sea and the sky . . . it's the most picturesque view in all of Southern California. I've driven across this bridge hundreds of times, but the beauty never ceases to amaze me, especially at night.

It's one of the best things being a military brat has given me. Naval Base Coronado is where we've called home for the past eight years. Unfortunately, I don't remember too much about the places we've lived before. We never stayed in one place long enough for it to matter.

Until now.

Eight years is the longest we've stayed put, and thankfully, it'll be my last move.

High-school graduation was last week, and while I should be enjoying my last summer before college, I'm not. The summer internship I applied for at Black Diamond Advertising expects me to start the Monday after graduation, which is today.

Since I grew up a military brat, most assume I would enlist as soon as possible. Many military brats do. Eh, no thanks. It's not for me. Instead, I come up with witty ideas and one-liners for various products, hoping to one day move on to more significant projects.

The sunrise is not as beautiful as the sunset over the bridge, but it's nothing I'll complain about. Squinting my eyes, I pull down the visor, reach for my sunglasses, then turn up the radio.

A little bit of rock, a few commercials I ignore, and some top hits later, I reach the parking garage in downtown San Diego, follow the designated signs, and pull into a spot marked for interns.

My nerves are on high alert as I walk through the front doors. The office lobby is crowded with many men and women dressed in business-casual wear. The scent of freshly brewed coffee hits my nose as I finally make it to the sign-in table. Quickly, I find my name tag, check a box on the form, and follow several others into a large conference room labeled for orientation.

Name tags dangle on the chairs. I circle the table until I find mine, then settle in. Slowly, the room fills up, and someone at the head of the table stands.

"Good morning, everyone. My name is Matthew, and I'm your boss, so don't upset me and you'll have a great time." There are a few chuckles scattered across the room. "I'm just kidding. Well, I am your boss, and my name is Matthew, but it's okay to upset me. In fact, I encourage it. Here at Black Diamond Advertising, we don't get anywhere by being cordial. Certain situations call for emotion, so bring it on." He's rewarded with a small round of applause. "Let's get to it, shall we? Jason, you're up." He tips his head toward the man to his left, who stands.

"Hi, everyone. I'm Jason, and I'll be your tour guide." He laughs. "Okay, maybe not, but I'm your guy if you need help with the numbers."

"Thanks, Jason. Now, we'll go around the table, and you can tell us your name and two fun things about you."

Fun things? What are we, in middle school?

Three people introduce themselves before I realize it's almost my turn. The person before me finishes, and quiet falls upon the table. *Shit*. I clear my throat.

"Sorry. I'm David. I'm a former military brat, spending the last eight years stationed at Coronado. The service life is *not* for me." Everyone laughs. "My passion is witty one-liners, and I have a thing for old black-and-white movies."

I retake my seat and listen intently as a few more go. There are a few more military brats in our midst, and we promise to swap stories later.

"Hey. I'm James. I grew up just a regular local city kid, born and raised. My grandpa was in the military, though, but my dad wasn't. Let's see . . . I like fast cars, spicy food, and now I feel like I'm on a dating site." The room fills with laughter again. "Taken, sorry, ladies." He shrugs, then takes his seat.

There's a knock on the door before it opens wide and the smell of coffee, donuts, and pastries fills the air. Matthew addresses the room one last time, gesturing to the assortment sitting on the opposite side. "Eat, drink, and be merry! Take some time to get to know one another. You'll be spending a lot of time together over the next several months."

Some immediately stand and head toward the back, while others remain seated. I glance around the room, eyeing the different personalities and styles reflected in my peers. Conversations around me flow seamlessly, and I find opportunities to immerse myself in them.

As I take a bite of my bear claw, excitement hums through my body. When not being asked why I want nothing to do with the military, I'm soaking in as much information as possible about the people I'm surrounded by. A smile tugs at the corner of my lips. Being creative, I never know where inspiration will come from, or what will spark my next big idea.

Chapter Two

James

"Come in, James." Matthew greets me when I walk in. "Take a seat; we'll start momentarily."

I nod, glancing around the conference room. It bustles with creative energy as I take a seat around the large table. Sunlight streams through the floor-to-ceiling windows, giving the polished oak surface a warm glow. This room exudes an aura of professionalism, with its sleek, modern furniture, interesting motivational posters, and shelves displaying the company's numerous awards and accolades.

A few familiar faces are around the table, but some I haven't met sit to my right. At the head of the table sits Matthew Daniels, a seasoned advertising executive known for his persuasive prowess. He's one of the main reasons I chose to work here—he's best friends with my grandfather, was a mentor to my father, and now, hopefully a mentor to me.

I look down at my clothes and wonder if I'm dressed appropriately. He cuts a fine figure in his charcoal-gray suit, burgundy tie, and black dress shoes. To Matthew's left is Jason Peterson, a sharp-minded market analyst sporting a crisp white shirt and navy-blue tie. To Matthew's right is an intern, David Sullivan. Out of the bunch at the table, he's the one who looks the most casual and artistic, donning a black leather jacket over a vibrant graphic T-shirt with black pants.

During one of the first intern luncheons, David mentioned he comes from a military background but wants to be as far away from it as possible. He seems like a rebel at heart, a creative innovator. His attire makes me feel more at ease in my khaki pants and polo shirt.

Anticipation floats in the air as we discuss the campaign for a new men's bodywash. Each person brings their perspective and ideas to the table, eager to leave a lasting impression on the executives and the client. Matthew is the first to speak.

"Ladies and gentleman, today we embark on a journey to redefine masculinity in personal care products. We need a campaign that resonates with the modern man, capturing his desire for self-care and confidence. To do so, we must have a bold approach."

"Matthew, I understand the need for innovation, but we can't forget the market research," Jason interjects. "Our demographic prefers authenticity and relatability over sensationalism."

"Ah, yes. I agree, Jason, but we need to make a brighter impact. We need to grab their attention and give them something to think about, something they've never seen before. That's where David comes in. He pitched his idea to me earlier this morning, and I think we should hear him out."

David leans forward, a mischievous glimmer in his eyes. "Imagine this: a series of ads featuring real men. Not your typical chiseled bodies, but ordinary guys showcasing their everyday lives. We capture their authentic moments, their challenges, their triumphs."

"It feels like everyone is doing that. The everyday male is not chiseled anymore—dad bods are in. So how do we ensure the product stands out among our competitors?"

With a smile, David continues. "We weave the product seamlessly into their stories, emphasizing how this bodywash enhances their experiences. Imagine a guy working a physically demanding job, covered in grime, but after using our bodywash, he emerges refreshed, revitalized, and ready to take on the world. It's about confidence, not just cleanliness."

I speak up. "It's more than just dad bods and some ad that looks real. It's genuine. It's empowering and engaging. I like it."

Matthew leans forward, his voice laced with conviction. "Jason, you and I know market research can't predict groundbreaking campaigns. We have an opportunity here to tap into the emotional core of our audience. This campaign will inspire men to take care of themselves, to embrace their vulnerabilities while remaining strong. It's not just about selling a product; it's about forging a connection."

Silence fills the room as Jason and Matthew exchange glances. Matthew's eyes light up at the audacity and brilliance of David's proposal—the potential to shift reality in men's personal care advertising.

Finally, Jason breaks the silence, a small smile tugging at the corners of his lips. "David, your vision is compelling. I see the value in tapping into the emotional realm while grounding it in authenticity. It's risky, but I believe it's a risk worth taking."

The conference room fills with a resounding yes as others, including myself, agree. I'm floored at David's idea and how quickly he won over Matthew and Jason. This is one guy I want on my side.

"Well, gentleman, we have a winning concept. This campaign will empower men to embrace their individuality and redefine what it means to be confident." Matthew claps his hands together. "Let's bring this vision to life."

Six hours later, we leave the conference room feeling energized, a sense of purpose and accomplishment fueling us forward.

Our new slogan: Revitalize yourself.

Chapter Three

David

THE EVENING AIR COMES alive with anticipation as I walk beside James, my colleague and newfound friend, into a vibrant bar that's pulsating with energy. It's been a couple of weeks since our successful collaboration on the men's bodywash campaign, and I'm quickly finding a new friend in James, both in the office and outside of it.

James waves to a beautiful woman standing outside the entrance. Her radiant smile lights up the dimly lit street. Her presence is becoming familiar, offering warmth and genuine friendliness. Tonight, she suggested a casual outing in a new bar that opened not too long ago to celebrate. We found out today that the client accepted our proposal of *Revitalize Yourself*, the colossal project we've taken on at work.

As we enter the bar, we're greeted with a lively atmosphere, clinking glasses, and laughter. It only adds to the noise level, competing with the cacophony from the dance floor. We settle into one of the only open booths, where the soft glow of candlelight hits the walls. James slides in first, then Jessica, leaving me on the other side.

Jessica's eyes gleam as she turns to me. "So, David, any special girls in your life? We haven't quite discussed that yet," she says playfully.

James chuckles. "Don't mind her—she's ever the matchmaker." She swats his arm in protest.

A smile tugs on my lips. "My focus has been on work. Unlike James, here, I'm simply an intern, not a shoo-in. Although, the world of romance seems to have eluded me for some time."

James chimes in, a teasing glint in his eyes. "Ah, come on. You're a creative genius! You must have left some fluttering hearts behind."

"Perhaps they're fluttering, but I've been too absorbed in the project to notice." I shrug. "Besides, who has time for love when we're conquering the advertising world?"

Jessica leans back into the booth. "Well, consider this a challenge, then, David. I have a friend I think would be good for you. She's intelligent, artistic, and she shares your passion for creativity. I'm confident you two would hit it off."

"A blind date?" I shift my gaze toward James, who shrugs. Jessica smirks, determination in her eyes. "Okay, count me in. But if this goes sideways, it's on you."

She reaches into her purse and pulls out a sparkly pink pen, then writes something on a napkin, tears it off, and hands it to me. It's a name—Raven—and a phone number. "Call her tomorrow afternoon."

Our conversation continues to flow as we sip our drinks, our laughter adding to the crowd's noise. James and I delve deeper into what we hope to accomplish at Black Diamond Advertising, the challenges we've overcome, and the impact we hope to make.

James comes from a long line of advertisers, while my military background helps me see things through a different lens. You'd think the military background would give me a one-up on the analytical side with a deep sense of attention to detail, but no. My mind goes the opposite way and dives into the boundless depths of creativity, allowing me to think outside the box. Our strengths complement each other, and I don't doubt that we'll be the dynamic duo of the company.

As the night progresses, I can't help but notice the chemistry between James and Jessica. They're high-school sweethearts, but there's a genuine affection that radiates between them. Even at nineteen, their relationship has a deep sense of understanding and unwavering support, something rare at our age. The more I glimpse into their life, the more I believe in the possibility of finding something like that for myself.

The evening wears on, the hours slipping away into the early morning. When we say our goodbyes, I realize the campaign we've been working on is about more than just revitalizing yourself. It's about strengthening the bond between two separate things that when combined become something magical.

"Thank you, Jessica, for bringing us together tonight. It's been fun." I give her a light hug.

She smiles as she pulls away. "You're more than welcome, David. I think this is the beginning of a beautiful friendship for us."

We reach the dimly lit street once again, this time more quietly. James hails a cab for them, and I head in the other direction.

As I walk the couple of blocks to my apartment, which I moved into a week ago, a weight seemingly lifts off my shoulders. Being a military brat, I've never had strong, tangible friendships. But tonight, I felt the shift. Not just the shift from military life to civilian, but the shift of reinventing myself and becoming the person I'm meant to be. Professionally, and personally, too—with fulfillment and the richness of deep connections I've never quite grasped before.

But also, I'm not going to lie—I am a tad excited at the prospect of a blind date. I didn't date much in high school, despite it being where we stayed in the one town the longest. I have a couple of friends, but it's all superficial. The kind you have in your childhood, not the lifelong type. This new chapter of my life, the new journey, will be shaped by friendship and love, and it's all thanks to a men's bodywash campaign. Now that's something I never thought I'd say.

With a sigh, I climb into bed, and the alcohol lulls me into a full night's sleep.

It's late afternoon when I realize I haven't called her yet. Sitting in my car after running to the grocery store, I pick up my phone and fish the piece of napkin out of my pocket. After dialing the number, I put the phone to my ear.

Raven's sweet voice greets me after five rings. I leave a detailed message with my name and why I am calling, then hang up and head back home to put the groceries away. As soon as I finish, my phone dings with an incoming text.

Raven: Hi, this is Raven. Sorry I missed your call. What's up?

Me: Hi, Raven. This is David. Not sure if you listened to my voicemail, but our mutual friend Jessica gave me your number and said I could call you for a blind date. Are you interested?

Raven: Yes! She did tell me to expect your call today. I'm free tomorrow night. What are you planning?

Me: Good to hear. What do you say we meet at the bowling alley on the corner of 56th and Main, around four? We can grab some dinner after if you're up for it.

Raven: That sounds wonderful. I'll be the one in a green hat with red hair.

Me: Perfect, see you then.

Chapter Four

David

THE SOUND OF BOWLING balls crashing against the pins reverberates through the bustling atmosphere of the bowling alley. I'm standing near the entrance, my heart pounding with nervousness and curiosity. This is the moment I've been waiting for—my blind date with Raven, the woman Jessica set me up with.

I scan the crowd down by the lanes. People cheer as a ball knocks out all the pins. Looking back to the door, my gaze lands on a figure that sorely stands out. Raven. She's dressed in a form-fitting dress, with white gloves that wrap around half her arms, and high-heeled shoes. Coupled with the green hat and bright-red hair, I'm surprised to see her face contorted into a disdained look as she glances around.

You've got to be shitting me.

I approach her with a polite smile, hoping to break through her initial reservations, and mine, too. "Raven, I presume? I'm David. It's a pleasure to meet you."

She glances at me critically. "Yes, I'm Raven. Pleasure is . . . yet to be determined," she says, her tone laced with sarcasm.

Undeterred, I extend my hand, hoping she recognizes the glimmer of optimism in my eyes. "Shall we give bowling a try? I'm a little rusty, but it should be fun."

Raven shoots a weary look toward the lanes. "Bowling? Really? I can't possibly imagine getting dirty with a bunch of germy balls and shoes. But since we're here, I might as well try."

Might as well try. Why did she think I invited her here if not to bowl?

Her resistance is apparent, but I'm determined to make the most of the evening. Maybe we'll end up having fun; who knows?

I secure our lane at the far end and grab our rental shoes. The clerk also hands me a pair of socks wrapped in cellophane. "For the lady," he says curtly. I nod.

I get it, dude. I'm surprised too.

Shoes tucked under my arm, I head to the concession stand and grab a chili cheese fries and two Cokes, then walk over to the table Raven just finished wiping down. I roll my eyes but don't say anything until she takes a fresh wet wipe and begins wiping down the seat in front of her.

"You a clean freak or something?"

"Something like that," she huffs, glaring at me. "What's that?" She motions to the package of socks on the tray.

"Oh, you'll need these for the shoes. They spray the shoes pretty well, but everyone is required to wear socks. If you don't have any, they provide these." I set the tray down and hand over the socks.

She plucks them from my hand and daintily slides off her high heels. Her feet hover as she puts on one sock and then the other, never touching the ground, as if it were made of lava.

I'd laugh if I knew she'd be okay with it. She doesn't look like she would be.

Chuckling, I slip out of my shoes and put the bowling shoes on. "Come on, Raven. It's just a little dirt, and as my momma always says, 'A little dirt don't hurt.'"

That earns me a laugh. "Your momma, huh?"

"Yep. Growing up a military brat, I couldn't fret about a little dirt. Dirt was a part of life. How about you?"

"San Diego, born and raised. My daddy owns a chain of hotels between here and New York."

Ah, that explains the whole Manhattan-socialite look she has going on.

"That sounds interesting. I like that. You ready to bowl?"

"If we must," she says.

"Don't sound too thrilled about it," I say, with a chuckle to lighten the mood. "The balls won't bite you."

Her response drips with condescension. "I'm not. I'm here out of a sense of duty to Jessica, who seems to believe we might actually be a match. How, I'm not sure, but I'm playing along."

"Wow, okay. Tell me how you really feel."

I walk over to the shelf of bowling balls behind me and pick out two, then place them both on the ball return and quickly gear up the pins. Still undeterred by her dismissive attitude, I pick up the heavier ball and demonstrate a smooth throw, sending pins flying with a satisfying crash. Four of the ten are still standing as the pinsetter resets them. After the ball returns, I throw it again, only knocking down two this time. It ends in a split.

The pins reset while I turn to Raven. "Your turn. Give it a shot; it might surprise you."

She delicately picks up the lighter ball in a dainty grip, her movements rigid and precise. Her throw lacks any real power, resulting in a slow roll that barely makes it halfway down the lane before hitting the gutter. I can't help but feel a mixture of frustration and disappointment. I wanted this to be a fun date. Bowling is fun. I wanted to give us a chance to connect, but for the life of me, I can't figure out why she agreed to the date in the first place if she didn't want to be here.

"That's okay; we can try again." I meet her at the top of the lane with another ball in my hand. I maneuver her fingers into the ball and position myself behind her. "Once your fingers are in the ball, you'll swing back your arm, like this." I run through the movement with her. "Then you'll swing it forward, throw it with force, and let go of the ball."

She drops it, and it thuds a foot away. She shoots me a glare.

"Well, not like that. You need momentum." I grab the ball and bring it back to her. "Think of it like a baseball bat. You have to swing it back before you can swing it forward to hit the ball. But instead of hitting it, you'll throw the ball down the lane."

She does it with more force this time, but it ends up in the gutter. She growls with frustration and tosses her hair back. "I don't like this."

Slowly losing my patience, I take my time phrasing what I want to say. "I understand this might not be your idea of fun. I'm wondering why you said yes to the date if everything feels gross and distasteful. Why are you here?"

"I told you. I'm here because of Jessica," she huffs. "This isn't my scene."

"Yes, but you could've suggested we do something different. What were you hoping would happen tonight?"

"Well, I assumed you were taking me to the art gallery a few doors down and didn't want to tell me. I didn't think we were actually going to *bowl* when you suggested we meet here."

My eyes widen. "There was no part of our conversation that mentioned an art gallery. I didn't even know there was one down the street." I run my fingers through my hair. "Isn't the point of a blind date to explore, have fun, and discover new connections? It's not about preconceived notions or surface-level judgments. It's about giving each other a chance and getting to know one another. An art gallery is not my idea of a good first date. Not that I don't love art—you just can't get a feel for a person in a stuffy gallery."

"Listen, David, I appreciate your candor and what Jessica's trying to do, but this isn't me. I'm used to a different lifestyle, one of elegance and refinement. I'm having even more reservations about how compatible we are."

"Fair enough. How about we make a deal? I won't force you to enjoy bowling, but you must promise to let go of your reservations, even just a little. Let's see where the evening takes us."

She pauses, thinking about it. "Okay. I'm willing to give it a try, but no guarantees."

As the rest of the night goes on, Raven makes more effort. Her grasps aren't as dainty and rigid, her throws get stronger, and she even throws me a smile when she finally knocks some pins down. Despite all her attempts, her patience quickly wears thin. She becomes increasingly frustrated and reverts back to her snooty manner. Any improvements quickly dissipate.

I can't help but feel disheartened by her lack of willingness to embrace the evening. While I have zero idea where she got the idea we were going to an art gallery, I wouldn't have minded if she'd suggested it. What bothers me the most is that she could've said something and chose not to. She chose to make this a horrible date.

Tension mounts between us with each turn we take, and after a couple more turns, I'm ready to call it quits. With a heavy sigh, I find the courage to tell her it's over. "Raven, I appreciate that you tried, even if the moment was fleeting. It's evident this just isn't working. We're not connecting, and it feels like we're forcing something that isn't meant to be."

She immediately removes the bowling shoes, tosses them toward me with the socks, and quickly slips back into her heels. "I couldn't agree more. This entire evening has been futile. Clearly, we're too different, and there's no point in pretending otherwise." She gives me a curt nod, grabs her purse, and quickly exits the alley.

What the fuck.

I head back to my apartment, only slightly defeated. It was only one date. One date with someone who just wasn't compatible. I won't say she's terrible—I don't know her, not really. An art gallery. Where in the world did she get that idea?

More importantly, though, was Jessica's judgment about me off? Or was there something else entirely that I missed or didn't consider? This was definitely a bad date for the books.

Chapter Five

David

AFTER THE LAST MISHAP, I have absolutely no idea why I'm letting Jessica send me on another blind date.

When I told her and James what happened between Raven and me the prior weekend, poor Jessica was horrified. Come to find out, she'd only met the girl a few times but knew her as an artsy, down-to-earth gal. That was far from the truth; how she got that impression is beyond me. It's the case of a mistaken identity. So, why I'm going on another blind date is anyone's guess. I don't have high hopes for this one, but I put on a good face and keep on trucking.

A pang of disappointment hits me after checking my phone for the tenth time. I've watched a few women walk through the front door of the arcade, but none of them have walked toward me. I told Ophelia, my second blind date, what I would be wearing so it would be easier to spot me. She said to meet her at seven, but at fifteen after, she still hasn't arrived. I send her a quick text before making my way over to the Skee-Ball machine.

Skee-Ball was one of my favorite arcade games when I was a kid. That and air hockey, but it's challenging to play when you're alone. I figure a game or two will help pass the time until she gets here.

I pick up three balls and aim for the targets. One hits the top of the cage and rolls into the lower circle. The second one hits the middle and gives me a hundred points, and just as I throw the third ball, there's a loud crash to my right. The ball flies out of my hand, veers off course, and lands in a neighboring lane, startling a woman.

"Hey, watch where you're throwing your balls! You nearly hit me." Her irritation is palpable as she storms in my direction.

"Woah, I'm sorry. I didn't mean to intrude on your game. It was a complete accident." I motion over my other shoulder. "I got distracted by the crash."

Her frustration softens as she studies my face. "Well, I suppose accidents happen. Just be more careful next time, okay?"

"Absolutely. I promise to be more mindful. Again, I apologize for the disturbance." I pull my phone out of my pocket, rechecking. It's now half past, and still no word from Ophelia.

"You know what?" she says, a small smile tugging at her lips as I tuck my phone back into my pocket. "You seem sincere enough. How about we make a deal? You can make it up to me by joining me for a round of mini golf. Consider it your chance to redeem yourself."

Momentarily stunned, I rock back on my feet. "Sure, that'd be great. It's the least I can do." I outstretch my hand and wait for hers. "I'm David."

"Kristie." She takes my hand and shakes it. "Let's go."

Our chance encounter turns into an exciting night. We step outside into the dusk and grab a basket of balls and two clubs.

"Ladies first," I offer.

She steps up to the tee, lines up the club, and makes soft contact with the ball—just hard enough to get it over the first bump.

"Nice shot." She steps aside, and I line myself up and take my turn. My ball lands farther than hers did, but when she gets it in the hole on her next shot, I know this will be a challenge. "Damn, you're good."

"Yeah. The benefit of growing up in a place like this." She shrugs and grabs her ball from the hole.

We quickly work on the next five holes, exchanging stories and laughing at each other's attempts to conquer the course's obstacles. Amidst the lighthearted banter, I find myself at ease with Kristie. She's warm and genuine, and she seems to have a real interest in me. It's both refreshing and enchanting. Her fingers rake light touches down my arms as she steps out of the way for me to hit the ball. She's got a zest for life that resonates with me. She's my kindred spirit.

With each hole we play, I feel myself growing fonder of her. I've never really believed in love at first sight and all that jazz, but there's something strong here. Kristie's unlike anyone I've ever known. Her competitive nature gives way to playful camaraderie as we cheer each other on and exchange friendly taunts when we miss the ball.

When we finally reach the last hole, I can't help but feel a tinge of disappointment, knowing the date is coming to an end, albeit vastly different from how the night began. She grabs the clubs and hangs them up, and I toss the balls back into the big bucket. "Kristie, today has been an unexpected adventure. I would have never guessed that a stray Skee-Ball throw would lead to such a wonderful outcome."

Her eyes sparkle with interest. "Definitely. I'm super glad we did this. Sometimes, the best things in life happen when we least expect them. I'm grateful you inadvertently found your way into my world today."

She intertwines her fingers in mine as I walk her to her car. She's parked on the other side of the lot, but I'm aching to spend more time with her already.

Before she climbs in the car, I speak. "To be honest, I came here tonight for a blind date set up by a friend, and I'm so fucking happy she stood me up." Kristie's eyes meet mine. "I'd like to see you again, Kristie."

I suck in a breath and wait for her answer. She smiles and grabs my front belt loops, pulling me closer, then stands on her tiptoes and plants a soft kiss on my lips. A kiss that electrifies me. There's a magnetic charge between us, forcing us closer. I wrap a hand around her waist and pull her close to my chest to deepen the kiss. Kristie moans when my tongue touches hers, and she opens her mouth a little more to let me in before pulling back.

"Give me your phone."

I pull it out of my pocket and hand it to her. She types away, and a moment later, I hear her phone ring. She hangs up and hands it back, saying, "There. Now you have my number, and you'll use it to call me tomorrow." With that, she winks and climbs into her car, leaving me speechless.

Her car leaves my sight before I walk down the lot to mine. I don't think I've ever been left speechless like that before. It's invigorating, and I'm hopeful for the future, hopeful of a future with Kristie.

Chapter Six

David

IT'S WEDNESDAY BY THE time Jessica checks in on me. I'm surprised it takes her that long, honestly. She was all over me for details about the last date.

Jessica: How'd it go?

Me: Don't I at least get a "Hey, how's it going?"

Jessica: Hey, how's it going? How'd your date go?

Me: Funny.

Me: It was amazing. I got stood up.

Jessica: How is that amazing?

Me: Because I met someone else.

Me: We played a round of mini golf and talked about everything under the sun. It felt good to connect with someone like that.

Jessica: What am I, chopped liver?

Me: Besides you and James.

Me: It was flirty and easy and fun. I'm going to see her again Friday night.

Jessica: Oooh, what's the lucky girl's name?

Me: Her name is Kristie Adams, and she plays a mean mini golf game.

Jessica: ...

Jessica: Kristie Adams? Blond curly hair, about my height, and has a freckle below her right eye?

Me: Yes ... Do you know her?

Jessica: What a small world!

Jessica: So, funny story. She's Raven's sister's boyfriend's twin sister. She was a year behind James and me in school.

Me: Indeed, it is.

San Diego is a big enough city, mainly if you include the neighboring suburbs. How interesting that they went to school together. None of the people I know now are people I went to school with. Granted, I did go to school on an island that serves as a revolving door for many families.

"So, I hear Ophelia stood you up."

I hiss when piping hot coffee splashes on my hand. "Dammit, man. You shouldn't sneak up on people pouring coffee." Turning on the faucet to rinse my hand off, I turn my head toward him. "Yeah, she did. But it's whatever." I wipe my hand and add creamer to my coffee.

"Can you imagine, though, you and her in bed? You moaning 'oh, oh, oh, Ophelia' to the tune of O'Reilly's

Auto Parts." James burst into laughter, slapping his knees. "I'm not sure how you could do that with a straight face!"

I chuckle. "Might've dodged a bullet with that one."

Jason pokes his head into the breakroom. "James, the numbers almost ready? I need those by 2 p.m."

"Yes, sir. Just finishing due diligence. It'll be on your desk by two o'clock."

"Well, better get back to it," I say, picking up my coffee and raising it in sympathy.

A blank sketchbook sits before me at my desk, waiting for me to pick up the pencil. Gray boxes fill out the left side of the board, rough sketches of designs. I'm flying solo, without a complete picture of James's market research. Sometimes, it's better to come up with a rough idea, then narrow it down with the research.

Designing an advertising campaign requires meticulous planning, strategic thinking, and a deep understanding of the target audience. It needs to create a message that resonates with the audience and leaves a lasting impression long after the campaign is over.

Skipping the market research, I dive into exploring various ideas and composites, pulling up the competitor to the product. Once you remove the demographics, desires, wants, and needs of the target audience, all you have left is the product itself and its placement within the research.

It's easy to take a picture of the product, place some text around it, and color it up, but that doesn't make it come alive. That's what I need—a bare-boned product at its simplest.

Once I have an idea of product placement, the pencil forms a mind of its own. It flies across the page, drawing circles within the gray boxes, then adding different shapes. After a while, the design loosely resembles a comic strip.

The once-blank canvas fills with ideas, each flowing into the next flawlessly until it reaches the end. Next, I draw lines to connect the different boxes, displaying more than one way to convey the story. Each storyline represents different selling points and emotions, some bigger than others.

Flipping the page over, I'm finally at my favorite part of the process: the slogans. I quickly write down the first five that come to mind, then immediately flip the canvas back over. The next time I'll review the opposite side is when the graphic designers make the campaign come to life.

It's a little superstition of mine—a lucky charm, if you will. They're five vastly different slogans, but all connected in some way, whether it's by a single word or it's the same word written in five ways. There has yet to be a campaign where we didn't use one of the slogans in some form. Sometimes, as a team, we combine two or three slogans to make a more impactful one.

A knock on the wall of my cubicle brings me out of my trance.

"Dude, you ready?" James stares at me, coat in hand.

I blink a few times. "For what?"

"Drinks with Anthony—his birthday."

"Shit, I forgot." I set my pencil in the cup to the right and quickly tidy up the rest of my desk. "Meeting went well?"

"Yep. The numbers are good, too, and we've defined the target audience. Still have some kinks to iron out, but we should be good by tomorrow's team meeting." James nods and puts on his coat.

"Perfect. I think they're going to like this one." With a grin, I take one last look at the full page in front of me, then slide it into the spot between my desk and the wall.

Chapter Seven

David

"I'M GOING TO MARRY her," I say between sips of beer. The sun dips below the horizon, casting a warm glow over the city skyline as we sit on the rooftop terrace at James's place. It's been a long day at work, but I can't contain my excitement any longer. I turn to James, who's looking at me with wide eyes.

"That's a huge step, David." He pauses, raising a brow. "Are you sure you're ready for it? Proposing is a life-changing decision."

I nod, keeping his gaze. "I know it's a huge commitment, but Kristie is the one. I've never had such a strong connection with anyone before. She brings out the best in me, and I want to build a future with her."

James leans back in his chair and takes a sip of beer. "I understand how you feel, man, but marriage will probably be the biggest commitment of your life. It's crucial to take the time to truly understand each other and ensure you're compatible in the long run. Have you discussed your future goals, values, and expectations? Like, what about kids? Does she want kids? Will she want to work or stay at home with the kids? And what about finances? Money is the number one issue couples have."

I shake my head, laughing. "Yes, of course. We've talked about kids, and I could go either way. She doesn't want kids right now—not a never, just not now—which is fine, because we're young. I want my career to take off before I have kids. Our goals and values align, and expectations come with time and evolve as you grow. Besides, I'm ready. I'd love nothing more than to settle down with Kristie and start our future together."

"I feel ya, man. I came from a broken home, and I know the effect it can have on a kid. Make sure you go into this knowing that marriage requires more than love. It's dedication, patience, understanding, and open communication. Make sure you're both on the same page before you take that leap."

Taking another sip of my beer, I let James's words soak in. He's right. Marriage isn't easy; I know that. But I did grow up in a household with two parents who never fought around me and always cared for each other. I'm sure others didn't have that luxury.

There are many aspects to consider, but we have the rest of our lives to figure it out. We'll hash out the important things and let the rest follow.

James's voice interrupts my thoughts. "You know Jessica will want to completely take over the wedding planning, right?"

A thunderous laugh rings out. "Oh, I have no doubt. She and Kristie will have a ball planning it. But as long as you're my best man, I don't care what they do with it."

"Of course, man. I'm honored you asked." He claps me on the shoulder. "Now, have you given any thought to how you'll propose?"

James signals to the bartender for another round, and I polish off the last of the beer in my hand. While we wait for our next round of drinks, I launch into the details.

We toss some ideas back and forth, and eventually land on a plan. My first stop tomorrow is to the jewelry store down the street from Black Diamond Advertising.

I'll scope it out during my lunch hour and see if anything catches my eye.

The more we talk, the more I realize it's been good to have James in my corner. He's sensible yet rational, something I definitely need to help curb my impulsiveness. We're polar opposites, yet somehow, our friendship works.

I've spent the last two months planning the proposal. Everything has to be perfect for my love. I'm a nervous wreck the night of, so much so that I asked Jessica to help make sure everything goes according to plan. Sadly, she wasn't as excited about my proposal to Kristie as James thought she'd be.

Since the first night I introduced them almost a year ago, Jessica has kept her distance. I've tried to ask Kristie about it, but she brushes me off, saying everything's fine and maybe Jessica doesn't want someone to take me away from her. Not that I am hers, but I'm her fiancé's best friend. Maybe she thinks I'd spend less time with them or something.

James says everything isn't okay, that Jessica thinks I'm too good for Kristie, but when you love someone, sometimes you need to trust them to make the right decision, and that's precisely what she's doing, albeit not happily.

The night has come, and I've pulled out all the stops. I made reservations at Kristie's favorite restaurant for a small booth in the back with twinkle lights strung around it to give it a soft glow. I preordered dessert and gave them a ring to sneak in there. Everything's perfect. All I need is my future bride-to-be.

When I see her walking toward me in the restaurant, my heart thumps in my chest. She's stunning in a little black dress, her hair pinned up like she's going to prom. "Kristie." I stand to greet her and kiss her cheek.

"Hi, David," she says breathily as she slides into the booth. "What's all this?"

"A nice dinner." I give her a gentle smile, attempting to mask how nervous I am. "I hope you don't mind, but I ordered us an appetizer."

"I wish you would've checked with me first. I hope you ordered the spinach and artichoke dip."

A sigh of relief flows through me. "Yes, as a matter of fact, I did."

"Good," she says, picking up the menu before her.

Not long after she sits down, our appetizer arrives, and the waitress takes our order. Kristie orders a chef's salad, and I order a steak. We make small talk until our food arrives, then we're mostly quiet.

She can talk my ear off, but weirdly enough, she doesn't talk much during meals. I'm learning to enjoy the silence. Tonight is not one of those nights. My leg jitters under the table as I wait for her to finish her salad. A moment later, the waitress comes with the dessert.

"Dessert?" She looks skeptically at me. "We never order dessert."

"Tonight is a special occasion." I meet her gaze and widen my smile, wiping my hands on the napkin, then address the waitress. "Thank you."

"Enjoy," she says, leaving us to nibble on the dessert.

The crème brûlée isn't my favorite, but I know it's hers. I offer her a spoon and motion for her to go first. She breaks the sugar and dips the spoon into it. Just as she brings it to her mouth, she stops.

"There's something in here." She taps the spoon on the small plate and fishes out the ring. "David?"

I take it from her grasp and dip my napkin into the cup of water, then wipe off the ring. "Kristie, I've known from the moment I met you that I wanted to marry you. Your smile brings me joy, and I want to see that smile every night before I go to sleep and every morning when I wake up. Will you do me the honor of being my wife?"

"Yes!" Kristie squeals as I slide the ring onto her finger, then she leans across the table and kisses me deeply.

Ahem.

Someone clears their throat, and she reluctantly pulls away from me.

"The check, sir." The waitress is blushing when I look at her. She puts the check on the table and scurries away. Pulling out my wallet, I count the twenties and place an extra two down for the tip.

Chapter Eight

David

Two years later...

Kristie sways her hips around the kitchen with a mop in her hand. She's wearing my headphones, singing along with the song on her phone. The sun shines through the windows, casting a warm ray of light on the freshly cleaned floors, and the faint scent of lemon fills the air. She moves throughout the kitchen, meticulously moving the mop back and forth with her back to me—she hasn't seen me come in yet.

"Kristie?" I call out before walking toward her. I tug the headphones from her ears at the exact moment she spins around and hits me square in the jaw with the mop handle. "Fuck!" I cry out and stumble backward.

"Oh, shit. David! You scared me." The mop clatters to the floor, and she rushes to my side. "Are you okay? Let me grab you some ice."

Holding my jaw, I walk to the dinner table and sit in my chair. Kristie comes back and holds the bag of peas against my face. "Ouch," I grumble. The coldness of the ice pack burns against my heated skin.

Looking around, I appreciate the work Kristie's done with the house today. "The house looks amazing. Thank you for grabbing that last load of laundry, too."

"Thanks, but I can't help but notice the trash is still sitting in the can." She gestures toward the overflowing bin near the back door. "I asked you to take it outside last night, and it's still here. Why do I have to do everything?"

I sigh. "It was an honest mistake, Kristie. I must've forgotten on my way out this morning."

She crosses her arms and glares at me. "It's not just about the trash, David. It feels like I'm constantly taking care of everything around here. I cook, I clean, I sweep and mop, and do the laundry when you forget. It's overwhelming. I need you to step up and take more responsibility."

"I'm sorry, I didn't realize taking out the trash was so important." I reach out and gently take her hand, needing reassurance as much as I try to reassure her.

"I hear you, and I want to help. Let's talk about how we can better tackle the household responsibilities."

She brushes my hand away and stands up, her brows furrowed. "Why should I have to tell you what needs to be done? Can't you see it for yourself? Shouldn't you take the initiative? You are the man of the house, are you not?"

Her words are like a punch to my gut. I take a deep breath while my brain catches up. "I'm not a mind reader, Kristie. I'm willing to help, but you need to communicate your needs so we can work together. That's what we talked about when you wanted a career change." She paces in a straight line to my left, and I turn to face her. "Neither of us can do everything. How about we devise a plan to establish a routine or system to ensure we share things? I can pick up a little extra while you finish school for your license."

Kristie's career change includes attending school for her realtor's license and a bachelor's degree in business. Classes take up most of her nights, and she spends her days at home studying, not working a day job. It's a significant change from being next in line to take over her father's arcade business. We've both had to make a lot of sacrifices to get this going for her, including my taking night classes to finish up my business degree while I work during the day.

Black Diamond Advertising offered me a full-time position straight after my intern summer. I gratefully accepted and have been working some twelve-hour days, then doing my classes after. It's been hard on our marriage, but I finished my degree early so Kristie could start hers and stop working for her father.

"I never agreed to that," she huffs. "You're misremembering it."

"How so?" I resist the urge to roll my eyes. How do I remember it incorrectly when we both stood in this kitchen and agreed I'd go first?

"I don't want to talk about this anymore, David. I'm tired."

"Then I don't want to hear anything else about not taking out the trash or helping you. I'm asking you to tell me what you want so I *can* help."

"I don't know what else you want me to say."

Running my fingers through my hair, I sigh. "I don't know either." Without saying another word, I stand up, grab the trash bag, and walk it to the can outside.

I hate the way she makes me feel sometimes. Hot, then cold. We're on, then we're off. It didn't used to be like this. She used to be so sweet, nurturing, easygoing, and considerate. My mind runs through our argument yesterday and how we left it unresolved.

It left me feeling helpless, not knowing how she wants me to help her. Yes, sometimes I overlook things like the trash. It was an accident—I didn't do it on purpose. I've had a lot on my mind with this new client.

Imagine a bridezilla for a CEO, but times it by two. That's how my new client is. Every idea I've had, she shits on. Even my best ideas are shit. Thankfully, no one has seen my slogans yet—the last trick up my sleeve.

It's not an excuse, though. But still, she's *that* concerned about the trash? I probably would've seen it when I came home from work and taken it out. We'll never know now.

The moments replay on a loop in my head, drifting to what happened after. Damn, the hold she has on me.

Her voice rings in my head. *"It's a wife's job to take care of her man when he's hurt..."* When I came back from taking out the trash, that's the first thing she said to me, then she whipped off her shirt and let her bra fall to the floor.

I groan but remember where I am and try to shake away the memory of me pounding into her from behind as she was bent over the counter. Her tits smashed against the marble countertop, her hair twisted around my fingers, my cock sliding into her slick entrance... It was one of the rare times she allowed me to fuck her from behind. It felt so good, but it was over too quickly. Three short moans fell from her lips, her pussy convulsed around my cock, and then she pushed me off her.

Fuck!

God-fucking-dammit.

Even now, the image of me fucking her over the counter has my cock standing at attention, even knowing she wouldn't let me finish. *"You're a big boy. You can do it yourself."*

It's like she's got my balls in a vise. I don't like it, not one little bit. A little power play, sure, but this? It's too much.

Maybe she's right. Maybe I need to take more initiative around the house. Maybe I do need to be more of a man.

With that resolve, I gather my things and head out of the office early to surprise her.

It's a short drive home, but when I get there, someone else's car is in my driveway. I park on the street and burst into my house. It's silent when I walk in through the door. "Hello?"

"David?" Her voice calls out from down the hallway. "What are you doing here?"

I walk into the kitchen and smack right into someone. "Who are you?" I roar as I look at the man I bumped into.

Kristie comes around the corner, tying her hair into a ponytail. "It's Chad. I told you about him the other day. He's over here studying with me for the test."

"Test?" I try to recall anything she's said recently about a man named Chad or an upcoming test when it clicks. I snap my fingers. "Oh, you're the man on the paper."

He finally speaks up. "Paper?"

"Yeah, the one with a phone number on it. I found it under a pile of papers on the counter the other day."

"You did?" Kristie's eyes widen.

I glance around the kitchen. "Where's the books?"

They both look around and then at each other. She's the first one to talk. "Oh, they're outside. It's such a beautiful day, I figured we'd study in the yard."

The blinds are drawn on the back door, so I make my way over there and open them. Sure enough, the table is cluttered with books and various papers. "Kristie, can we talk in the bedroom for a moment?"

I'm not about to let some classmate ruin my resolve. She nods and holds a finger up to Chad, signaling she'll be a minute.

"Take your time," he says.

As if I'd do anything else. This is *my* house.

She follows me into our bedroom, and when the door softly closes behind her, I pounce, trapping her between my chest and the door. I breathe in her scent and groan. "I've been thinking about you all day." My lips meet her neck, and she draws in a sharp breath.

"We have company out there."

I nibble on her neck and then soothe it with my tongue. She ducks out of my grasp.

"What do you want, David?"

"I want you," I growl.

"I'm not going to fuck you with someone in the living room. Now please, let me out."

"Kristie." I turn around to face her. "Please. I need you."

She pauses, briefly considering it. Then, her hand flies up to caress my cheek. "That's my big boy." She stands on her toes and brings me in for a kiss. I reach for her tits and grab a nipple through the material.

"Not yet," she whispers, running a hand down the length of my cock. "Let me take care of you."

My dick hardens instantly, craving her attention. She unbuckles my belt and lowers my pants, freeing my cock. She gets a glimmering look in her eye as she darts her tongue out and runs it along the shaft, then finally takes me in her mouth.

Pleasure ripples through my body. Her mouth hasn't been on me in *months*. "Oh, Kristie."

No sooner had I moaned her name than she removed me from her mouth. She stands up and heads to the door, opening it slowly. "There's your start. We have company. Don't forget to turn on the shower while you finish."

The fucking audacity.

Chapter Nine

David

JAMES AND I STUFF the last boxes into the U-Haul he rented. It's bittersweet, him and Jessica moving across the country. Well, to Kansas, so halfway across the country, but it still applies.

Don't get me wrong—I'm happy for them. I'm just going to miss my best friend. We've been the dynamic duo at work for so long; it won't be the same without him. The space already feels emptier, and he hasn't even left yet.

"Man, I'm going to miss this," James says between breaths.

"I know what you mean." I nod. "It's going to blow balls now that you're leaving."

Jessica walks out of the apartment and hands us a couple of beers. "Take a breather. It's hot out here."

I chuckle as I watch Jessica shift in the chair, trying to get comfortable, then she rests a hand on her belly.

"I can't believe I'm going to miss this little bug growing up," I say to them.

James shakes his head. "You won't miss anything, promise. She'll send you so many baby pictures that it'll seem like you're there."

"As long as I don't have to see the birth, I'm good." I take a sip of my beer.

"Eww, I don't even want to see the birth, and I'm the one who has to do it!" Jessica sighs but smiles.

She's two months pregnant, and I was the first one to know. I accidentally walked into my bathroom and found her staring at the stick in her hands. We have a guest bathroom for a reason, so it wasn't like I expected to be walking in on her. I stepped out just as quickly as I entered, but she ushered me back in and threw the pregnancy test at me. Then she threw a second and third one at me like she couldn't contain her excitement.

Of course, because I knew first, it had to be a secret. She roped me into helping her plan something special for James for the announcement, saying it was the *least* I could do with making her help Kristie with the wedding and whatnot. Jessica's like the sister I never had—I could never deny her.

She breaks the memory. "When are you and Kristie having babies?"

James snorts. I shoot him a glare. *Shut up, man.*

"When are we doing what?" Kristie comes out from behind Jessica, holding a margarita.

"Babies!" Jessica squeals. "My little one is going to need a cousin or three."

Kristie polishes off the drink in one gulp. "Oh, hell no! No babies are going to fuck my figure up."

Jessica's jaw drops. We'd talked about having kids someday, but I guess she chose for us. I wish I could say her words shocked me, but they don't. Lately, she's been making more decisions for us with absolutely zero input from me.

"David, I thought you wanted kids?" James takes a sip of his beer. He knows damn well I do.

"Eventually, yeah, I'd like a kid of my own." I don't dare look at Kristie, because I can see the smoke coming out of her ears from here.

He downs the rest of his beer and stares at Kristie. "Well, there's no time like the present!"

We all laugh except for Kristie, who walks back into the apartment and slams the door, causing the windows to rattle.

"Damn, who pissed in her Cheerios?" James says as I walk toward the front door. I shake my head, then enter the apartment, searching for Kristie, following the sound of sniffles. She's in the back bedroom, holding a tissue up to her nose.

"It was a joke . . ."

"It's not a goddamn joke, David. You know good and well I don't want kids," she sneers at me.

"No, actually, I don't. We've always talked about having them someday." I run my fingers through my hair.

"I don't know what you're talking about." She sniffles into the tissue again. "You're all against me, and I don't appreciate it."

I advance toward her and pull her into my arms. "I'm sorry. We're not trying to go against you; we were just talking."

"It's your fault they hate me." She takes a step back to face me. "Thankfully, they're leaving, so we won't have to deal with them anymore."

My fists clench at my sides. Take shots at me? Fine. Take shots at my friends? You've got another thing coming.

"Kristie, I've told you before. They don't hate you; they just don't like the way you treat me sometimes. Besides, you're my wife. You'll always come first."

A sly smile tugs at her lips, and I know I've appeased her, for now. "Come on. I'll duck into the bathroom, then let's get back out there. We're almost done," I promise her.

She stops me in the doorway. "No."

"No? No, what?"

"You can't go to the bathroom."

"Excuse me?" I shake my head, not sure I heard her correctly.

"You heard me. Hold it."

"My piss? I'm not going to hold it. I'm going to the bathroom." Another couple of steps, and she's right at my side. "Kristie, what are you doing? This isn't funny."

She shoves me into the bathroom and then closes the door, turning me around. "Neither is the way they treat me. Hold it five minutes."

"What are you talking about? Nobody treated you any kind of way. Now move, please, so I can piss." I rub my fingers against my forehead. I'm over her games right now.

Crying one minute because James makes a crude remark, and bossing me around the next, telling me when I can and can't take a piss. What the fuck is this?

Slap!

Her open palm hits my cheek, causing me to hiss and step backward. My back hits the door.

"What the fuck, Kristie?" She's never raised a hand at me before. I cradle my cheek and glare at her. "Get out!" My hand fumbles for the doorknob behind me, finally managing to twist it open.

"Your five minutes are up anyway. Have fun peeing, big boy." She winks at me and smacks my ass as she strolls out of the bathroom.

Chapter Ten

David

FOUR YEARS LATER...

A fresh start is exactly what we need. We've made San Diego our home for quite some time now, but it's getting a little boring. James has been keeping in touch and has a new position open as VP of Creative Solutions for his company. Honestly, I jumped at the opportunity.

I've been making the rounds at Black Diamond Advertising, but I know I'll never reach the top, which is what I'm striving for. So, when James presented me with the job offer *and* gave me an expense account for moving, it was an easy decision.

Besides, Kristie has been unemployed for the last year and a half and is blacklisted from almost every realty company in the city. But who's counting?

Okay, fine, I'm counting. It's been the worst year and a half of my life.

We've been back and forth. We've been up and down. We've been happy and depressed.

She calls it quits; I beg her to stay. She wants to stay; I want her gone.

Love's a battlefield of eggshells, and I feel like I'm the only one hurting.

Of course, she doesn't want to move—even that's a fight—but at this point, it's necessary.

I'll never forget the day she told me why she got fired. Some barely legal college intern was caught with his hands up her shirt. A man's hand up a woman's shirt isn't a big when both parties are of age and are consenting. But there's no consent when she's his boss and in a position of authority. Allegedly, she coerced him into touching her breasts because he was a nerdy virgin. She says he was blackmailing her into letting him touch her, or he'd tell Kristie's boss she was freely giving blow jobs to the interns—which is a load of bullshit if I ever heard it. She *despises* giving head. He claims Kristie threatened to fire him if he didn't sleep with her. Once the CEO heard about this, he fired her immediately.

I don't blame the guy. I know how she is, and I also know how horny college boys can be. Only the two of them truly know what happened. She claims nothing ever happened between them—he's too young, she's his boss, something about "molding his young mind."

In the end, it doesn't matter who is right; it only matters what it looks like. From an outsider's perspective, it doesn't look good. The CEO was right to fire her. And once word got around, no other agency wanted her.

So here we are. Moving to Crimson. Hopefully, this will be a blessing in disguise. I've even gotten her to agree to marriage counseling to help us resolve some of our issues.

Where I come from, you don't cheat or get a divorce. You work your shit out, and if you can't do it together, you see a professional. Us Sullivan men take our vows seriously. We're in it until death tears us apart.

Despite all the crap she's done through the years, there's still a tiny part of me that wants the old Kristie back. The one I dated, the one I fell in love with. I want to go back to the days when she'd pack my lunch, and I'd leave the coffee pot on for her in the mornings.

Dating her was easy, but I think that's the point. Dating is easy. It's fun. You spend some time together, and at the end, you go your separate ways, back to the comforts of wherever you call home.

Marriage is a whole other world. You see each other all the time, and your personal quiet space is now shared under the one roof. You become annoyed with the quirks you used to adore. You fight over whose turn it is to wash the dishes or take out the trash. To marry and love someone is to continuously choose them every day, even when it feels like you can't. You have to make that decision every day, and remind yourself that not every day will be rough. Not every day will end in frustration.

It'll be great to be around friends again. Kristie doesn't let me have company around too often these days. It's usually just us in our small house, and lately, I'm dreading coming home from work.

I finish taping up the last box from our guest bedroom and take it with me into the garage. Moving day isn't for a couple of weeks, but it's easier to start packing the things we won't need between now and then.

Kristie's sitting on the couch with her feet up on the coffee table when I come back in from the garage. "Done yet?" she says, not looking up from the TV show she's watching.

"The guest room is packed and staged in the garage." I plop down next to her and outstretch my arm around her shoulder.

She flinches at the touch and scoots away as though I've burned her. "Ew, you need a shower. You're all sweaty and gross."

"Come shower with me." I stand up and hold out my hand. "I'll make it worth your while."

"No thanks," she huffs, her lip curling in disgust.

Sometimes, I just want to shake the ever-loving shit out of this woman and ask her what the fuck is wrong with her.

Chapter Eleven

David

SIX MONTHS LATER...

"Who are you?"

Her voice startles me, and I look up from the TV.

"Sky, mind your manners." James walks into the living room with his beer. "Pick up your backpack and come meet my friend."

She does so, but her hazel eyes zero in on me, then she backs up toward James. "It's okay, James." I turn to greet her formally. "Hi. I'm your Uncle Davey."

"I don't have an Uncle Davey," she spits out, her gaze unwavering.

I chuckle and raise my hands in surrender. James explains how we know each other.

"But my friends call me Davey. We can be friends, can't we, Bug?" I stick out my hand and wait.

She tilts her head, thinking, before she places her hand in mine and shakes. "Sure, as long as you get out of my spot."

I look around and realize I must be sitting in her spot on the couch. Standing up, I let out a thundering laugh. "I think this is the beginning of a beautiful friendship."

The rest of the night goes by quickly. My new friend doesn't leave my side, even when I yell at the TV and make frustrated noises because the ball keeps getting intercepted. Damn guys can't keep the ball to save their lives.

Once Sky gets tucked into bed, I let everything out. I can't keep it in.

"She's just so infuriating!"

"What's the problem this time?" James takes a sip of his second beer.

"She treats me like shit, James. Kristie would have a fit if she knew I was talking to you about this."

"Kristie treats everyone like shit—has for as long as I've known her."

"I know, but she's my wife, man." I sigh. If it's not one thing, it's another. Between sharing my location twenty-four seven, keeping within a certain radius from home and work, and always being on a short leash, I wonder if this marriage is worth it. If she even wants this to work. "I wish she would love me the way I love her—unconditionally, willing to go the extra mile to put a smile on my face, or just wrapping her arms around me for a warm hug. A phone call or a text when she's running late, maybe pick up my favorite beer on the way home from work or plan a date night for us. Damn, give me a *little* something to show you care."

It's more than that, though. She's slowly sucking the life out of me, and not in a good way.

The garage door opens, and heels click on the floor a moment later. Jessica comes into view and makes small talk with us before she heads off to bed, insinuating James better hurry along if he wants to get laid tonight.

"You can have that kind of love too, you know," James says. "It's not about being possessive, bitchy, and high maintenance. It's about the mutual respect you have for each other, admiration, and the understanding that the two of you are in this for the long haul. Sadly, Kristie doesn't have those traits, and unfortunately, I don't think she ever will."

As I pull into my driveway, I think about how James's statement hits a little too close to home. A light flickers on upstairs, filling my heart with dread.

I know I stayed at James's a little longer than I planned, and when I walk into the still air of my kitchen, I sigh. Opening the fridge, I grab a bottle of water, uncap it, and take a sip, then head upstairs to face Kristie.

She's waiting for me when I open our bedroom door, and she looks unhappy.

"You're late."

It's all I can do not to roll my eyes. I know I'm late, according to her. It's barely 10 p.m. She walks across the bedroom and steps in front of me before I can make it to the bathroom. "Excuse me," I say.

She doesn't move, just keeps holding her stance.

"What are you doing? I need to piss."

Her eyes darken, unblinking.

"Hold it. Fifteen minutes."

I try to step around her, and she slaps me. Then she looks at her watch. "I said, you can hold it."

Holding piss in hurts. She knows I'd rather die than piss my pants in front of her. Sadly, this is just one of her punishments.

The seconds tick by slowly, but as soon as the time is up, she steps to the side, and I burst into the bathroom, slamming the door behind me.

A few minutes later, as I'm brushing my teeth, there's a knock on the door. "Go away, Kristie." I don't bother hiding my disgust.

"I'm not done with you yet."

God-fucking-dammit.

"Not tonight." How the hell she expects me to fuck her after that is beyond me.

"Yes, tonight. I've been waiting for you all night. So get out here, big boy, and come claim your prize." She flings open the door and poses awkwardly over the doorframe, then saunters over to reach for my cock, running her fingers down my length.

Toothpaste hits the sink, and I rinse out my mouth. Resigned, I walk her backward until the back of her knees hits the bed. I lean in to kiss her, but she stops me, puts her hands on my chest, and pushes me back. She points to the bed, daring me to speak.

I stay silent, obeying her unspoken commands, and I'm rewarded with soft lips as she peppers kisses on my chest. Slowly, she makes her way down to my boxers, then stops. *Keep going* . . . I nudge her head down, but she cocks it to the side and glares at me.

"Not today, big boy."

Not any night.

She pulls my boxers down to reveal my erection—the one I don't want. My body is reacting to her touch and only her touch.

"My, my. Someone is excited." She straddles me and reaches between her legs, spreading some of her wetness onto my hard cock. Then she teases my tip against her slit.

"Kristie . . ."

I groan as she lowers herself on to me. She rocks back and forth, leaning forward to shove her tits in my face. Reaching up, I squeeze one, twisting one of the nipples the way she likes. In no time, she's almost at her climax, and I'm nowhere near the finish line.

Crossing my fingers that she'll let me finish, I sit up, grab the base of her neck, and tangle my fingers in her hair. Arching her back, I pump in and out. "Fuck."

Her breaths falter, and she moans. But before I'm able to come, she climaxes.

"Sorry, big boy. The only way you're coming tonight is in that bathroom." She climbs off me and quickly climbs underneath the covers.

"Come on, Kristie. Help me out." I'm pleading, but it's not the first time she's done this.

"You've been a bad boy, and bad boys don't get help to come."

What a bitch. I take a deep breath, get off the bed, and grab a clean pair of boxers before entering the bathroom. Just like that, she's done with me for the night.

Unfortunately, my cock didn't get the memo. He's still standing at full attention, aching to be released. Turning on the shower, just like she demands, I will my cock to go down. With a degraded heart, I grab my phone and navigate to my favorite porn site. Her juices still coat me, but I squeeze some lube into my hand anyway.

After I prop my phone against the sink, I rub my hand up and down, wishing she'd let me do all the dirty things I crave, all the dirty things she snubs her nose at. I'd love to shove my cock down her throat and make her choke, or to fuck her warm, wet pussy from behind. Then, just as I imagine sliding in and out of her, I come, stifling my groan with a towel, just like she demands.

By the time I shower, dry off, and re-dress, she's nowhere to be seen. What greets me is my pillow on top of a blanket—the key indicator I'm sleeping on the couch tonight.

After flipping the channel to a replay of tonight's game, I ponder where exactly our marriage went wrong and how I became an unwilling participant in her games. Something James said rings in my head, hitting a little too close to home as I fall asleep. *"You can have that kind of love too, you know."*

Chapter Twelve

Kristie

HE TRIES TOO HARD, the poor guy, although it's comical to watch at times. Truly, I wish things were different, but they're not.

He's not the man I want him to be despite being wrapped around my finger. David will do anything I say, anything I want. He wants so much to please me, to be a good boy.

I tend to my wifely duties when absolutely needed, cockblock him when I can, and do whatever else I see fit.

And by whatever, I mean whomever.

My newest little toy's name is Jacob. The best thing about Jacob? He'll walk over hot coals whenever I demand. The second-best thing about Jacob? He works directly under my lowly husband.

Two men are at my disposal, and neither of them has my heart.

Poor David. He tries. I know he does. But I need more—something he can't give me. It's not a matter of physicality, it's a mentality. I don't think he understands it or knows it's beneath the surface—this overwhelming desire to hurt him, to punish him, to make him worship me.

So why did I plan a surprise birthday party for him and rope Jessica into it? God only knows. She's letting me use their house despite our wobbly friendship. She hasn't liked me since the day she met me, and honestly, I don't blame her. I'm the type of woman who needs a man to pay attention to me and only me. I'll be your closest friend, your family, your lover, your everything. I tolerate her because of David. The part of me that aches to claim him knows he won't break his friendship with James and her.

This is a nice thing she's doing, though. She basically did everything, from the cake to the decorations. I didn't have to lift a finger. She invited his coworkers and coordinated all the minute details, just like I let her do with my wedding. I couldn't have cared less if we went to city hall and signed the damn papers. I was easy in that sense—faking it the whole way. I spent Daddy's money like a good girl, bought all the fancy things, and snagged me a husband, but none of it was really me.

I take another long drag of the cigarette and let out a slow breath. It's a nasty habit, yes, but sometimes nasty habits are necessary. Just as I finish my smoke, I hear little Sky running around the house, telling everyone it's time for cake.

Good. Time for my present.

While everyone is in the living room singing Happy Birthday to David, I sneak up behind Jacob and nibble on his ear. "I'll let you fuck me if you can catch me."

He immediately spins and reaches for me. His fingers graze my arm when I sidestep him and dash down the hallway toward the guest room in the back.

I haven't even entered the bedroom before I rip my shirt over my head. Anticipation pools between my legs as I strip the rest of my clothes and climb on the bed to kneel facing the headboard.

The door opens a moment later, and I hear a low whistle.

"Well, come on, little one. We don't have a lot of time." I look over my shoulder and see him pushing down his pants in a hurry. His dick bounces with his movements, and he positions himself behind me. His left hand twists my nipple as he uses his right to guide his length inside me. I let out a low moan and feel him slide balls deep.

"Damn, you're wet, baby."

"Shh, don't talk."

Jacob fucks me slowly and deliberately, like it doesn't matter if we're in someone else's house at my husband's birthday party. I like how it gets him off—knowing he's fucking his boss's wife. His lips meet the nape of my neck, and he sucks, then moves to the other side. I grab his other hand and smash it against my tit. He holds both of them while he fucks me, slowly picking up speed.

I need more. Harder. Faster. Rougher. Submit to me, little one. Worship me.

"That's it?" I breathe. "Come on, you can do better than that." The bed moves slightly with each thrust. "Oh, that's it. What a good boy." He groans at my words. "Yesss."

His teeth graze my neck again, biting this time, then he licks the spot tenderly. I reach a hand between my legs to strum my clit, bracing myself against the headboard with my left hand. I need to come, desperately. Every nerve in my body is hyperactive, and I'm positive I'll combust if I don't come. Small whimpers leave my mouth. "Right there, little one." I'm just about there when I hear it.

"What the *fuck* is going on?"

Jacob continues his thrusts inside me. I turn my head again to look over my shoulder and meet his wide eyes. I flash him a wicked smile. At the exact moment I reach for the sheet, Jacob pulls out and covers my ass with his gross, sticky mess. I cover myself up and slide my ass along the bed, ridding myself of Jacob's release.

"David, I was just . . ."

He leaves, slamming the door behind him, and a lamp crashes to the ground and breaks. I pull on my shorts and T-shirt, leaving my bra discarded on the ground.

"David, wait," I yell, pushing someone out of my way and rounding the corner after him. "David!"

He stops short of the front door and addresses me with a venom I've never seen. I like it. "No, Kristie. We're done." He opens the front door only to slam it behind him.

I watch David get into his car, mentally kicking myself, and by the time I'm down the driveway, he's already gone.

Goddamn it.

He ruined my fucking orgasm.

Chapter Thirteen

David

I WAKE UP TO a fierce pounding in my head and my left arm in a sling. James sits next to my bed, reading the newspaper.

"Son of a bitch," I groan as I struggle to sit up.

"Take it easy, man. You were in an accident," James says.

My mind drifts to the events of last night. Everything after drinks at the Twilight Club is a blur.

Finding Kristie fucking Jacob, and the look in her eyes . . . Yeah, we're completely over. There's no coming back from that. Ever.

I'm not sure what time it is when I wake up, but when I do, James is gone. I adjust the bed to sit up more, then close my eyes again.

Kristie's voice was the last thing I wanted to hear, but here she is. She walks toward me with a cup of water and helps me drink it. I try to swat her hand away, but

I'm still groggy from the medicine they gave me to help me sleep. She sets the cup down after I take a few sips. Her wedding ring flashes before me, and my mind reels back to last night.

"Kristie." I reach out and grab her hand. She looks at me with a strange look in her eyes. "I want you to go."

"I'm not leaving you, but I will leave you wanting more. I'm the best you'll ever have." She winks and runs her hand down my chest.

My chest heaves as I struggle to breathe. "You cheated on me. You let another man fuck you while you were wearing my wedding ring. We're done. It's over."

"You're overreacting. When my man is hurt, it's my job to take care of him." She looks toward the door to verify it's closed, then turns back to me and snakes her hand under the blanket.

"Kristie, stop."

She leans into me and whispers, "I want to take your hard cock in my mouth and suck. Let me make you feel better." Her hand slides up my hospital gown as she kisses my neck.

I groan and feel like I'm being torn in two. She strokes me a couple of times and kisses me. I'm fully erect, even though I despise her right now. Our sex is hate-sex. It's never loving or romantic. I hate it. I hate how my cock enjoys the attention.

"I said stop. Leave, Kristie."

Without taking her gaze off me, she tightens her grip on my cock, reminding me she's in control. Then she moves the blanket, lifts my gown, and sucks my tip into her mouth, making me gasp. *Oh, fuck. This feels good.* I can't remember the last time she sucked me off.

My head is at war with my cock. She fucking cheated on me! I'm enraged as her mouth slides up and down my cock. I push her head down hard and fist her hair as she gags. I let her mouth slide up a little, just enough to breathe, then force her head back down again.

Yes. God, it feels good to be in control.

"Take it. Fucking take it, bitch." She looks up at me with glistening eyes, almost pleading with me. I hold her head in place and thrust my hips up, ramming my cock down her throat, fucking her mouth with a smirk on my face. Saliva runs down her chin and hits my balls.

She cheated on me. The thought hits me square in the chest again. She squeezes my balls a little, and I drag her off me, only to shoot my cum on her face.

There's a knock at the door, and the nurse enters the room before Kristie can enter the bathroom.

It's been almost four years to the date since I face-fucked Kristie. The first week was interesting, to say the least. I had one week of quietness, one week of contemplation, and one week of confirmation I'll never go back.

I moved my belongings into the Wyatt's house and refused to talk to her until after I served her divorce papers. With each day that passed, I felt lighter. Every week that goes by is another week I'm stronger. One month turns into another, then into a year, and before I know it, it's been almost four years.

Slowly, I start coming back to life. Jessica's showing me various ways to cook and how to enjoy it. James drags me to the gym with him, and I'm losing weight—including the hard shell I created around me to withstand the abuse. One of my favorite things to do now is run early in the morning. At the start of high school, Bug decided to join cross country and championed me as her running partner—not that I mind. It's nice to have someone by your side who understands the importance of stopping at the park by the lake and watching the sun come up over the water. There's something special in knowing the sunrise brings a brand-new day.

Oh, my Bug. She brings light to my life in the best ways and is the best cheerleader. She challenges me in ways I never imagined. Our family dinner time is special to the four of us. We'll debate over silly topics—sometimes serious, but mostly not—or we'll play a game of slapjack. I like turning the heat on her. Red suits her well and draws out a spark within her. She comes alive.

The way I catch her staring at me sometimes makes me chuckle. She doesn't know I've noticed it. Her sweet sixteenth birthday was a couple of weeks ago, and I get the feeling she's developed a little crush. Harmless, really. Until I catch her staring at me more often than not.

Then I start to pay more attention to the little things. The way she sneaks glances at me when we're at the lake. The way she'll go out of her way to do things for me, and the way she lets me catch her gaze making its way down my body. She was such a sweet little girl, and now she is becoming a sweet woman.

Never in a million years would I let something happen between us. It's flattering to know I still have it despite my marriage to Kristie. Her stolen looks give me the confidence to start dating again.

I've met Julie a handful of times. Crimson is a small town, and she works at the bookstore in the plaza. We met for coffee and had a good conversation. I take the plunge and ask her to go to a club with me, figuring we'd go dancing and see where the night leads.

Only, it doesn't go anywhere, because who does my date literally run into? Bug. Our night is cut short when I drag Bug out of the club and shove her into the car in her tight little red dress that doesn't leave much to the imagination.

Chapter Fourteen

James

Two years later...

I do a double take as David rounds the door of Sky's room.

"*What the fuck?* Sky. Skylar!" My voice echoes down the hall. "Get out here, now."

My best friend is shirtless, with his pants unbuckled at his waist. There's no mistaking what just happened.

My chest heaves as I shove him against the wall and hold him with my forearm.

"James? What's wrong?" Jessica runs up the stairs and stops at the top. She looks at him, then to Sky, then to me, back to him, back to her, finally resting on me. "Oh."

"It's not what it looks like," he starts, but I push into his chest a little more with a threatening look. I hold up my other hand and wave Sky toward me to inspect her. She takes a couple of steps but stops short.

"Dad, I . . . I can explain." She glances down at the floor.

"This fucker better not have hurt you!" I say as I turn toward Jessica, who rushes to Sky's side.

She brushes her mother off, saying, "I'm fine."

"The hell you are!" I yell as I let him go, only to spin around and punch him square in the jaw. "What the *fuck* have you done?"

"Dad! Stop!"

I trusted him. I brought him into my home and trusted him to do right by me. My fist meets his stomach, and he doubles over. "You are nothing! Nothing!"

"Hold on. James, wait." He scrambles to his feet.

My fist meets his jaw again. "I swear to God, if you hurt my little girl, I'll kill you! Get the fuck out of here!"

He mumbles an apology to my girl, and my face burns.

"Don't you ever talk to her again. Don't even look at her. Don't come back here. I'll kill you, you bastard! I'll kill you!"

The front door slams a moment later. I start to head down the stairs but change my mind. Instead, I charge at my little girl. When I reach her, I lift one of her arms and then the other. "What did he do to you? Did he hurt you?" I spin her around and try to lift her shirt.

"James," Jessica whispers behind me, barely penetrating my fury.

"That motherfucking asshole! I'll kill him."

"Leave him alone, Dad. He didn't do anything wrong." Tears stream down her face.

"He touched my baby girl!" Heat radiates off me, and she flinches at my words.

"James."

"What?!" I whip around to look at my wife.

"You don't know what happened. Take a breath." She takes a step toward me.

"He touched my baby girl, Jessica. There's no coming back from this."

It's been a week, and my hands still fucking hurt. It doesn't help matters that I bought a punching bag and hung it up in the garage. But what hurts the most is the betrayal. My heart is fucking shattered.

How did I not notice what was going on under my roof?

How did I not notice the changes between them?

Goddamn it. She's my baby girl!

After everything I've done for him.

All the hours building each other up, all the beers, all the good and bad times. This is how he repays me? By sleeping with my daughter behind my back? For God's sake, she's barely eighteen. Still a baby! My baby.

I can't get the image out of my head. The image of him hurting my little girl, touching her—whether consensual or not. Sky claims it was consensual, but how do I know he didn't coerce her into it?

I'll never understand this. How could he have taken such an advantage at the expense of our friendship? Out of all the women in Crimson, why did he have to fuck my daughter? I can barely look at her now. I'm so disgusted at the mere thought of him touching her. I thought I knew him better than to touch my baby. How well do you really know someone, anyway? Someone who is supposed to be your best friend, someone who has been a brother to me for over twenty years. Someone I've looked up to, someone I mentored.

Over the past week, Jessica's tried to talk to me numerous times. She had a lengthy discussion with Sky, who admitted she came on to him and he pushed her away. She told Jessica that's why he moved out two years ago, and that's why he's not around much now either. *Two fucking years.*

Not once in those two years did he say anything to me. Not once.

The fucking nerve of this guy.

Sweat drips down my back as I swing my fist into the bag. It rattles against the chains but barely sways. The garage door open behinds me and slams shut a moment later.

The person in my garage is the last person I ever expected to be here.

David.

I turn to face him head-on. "I thought I told you to leave and never come back."

"We need to talk."

"No, we don't. You fucked my daughter. You're lucky you're not dead yet." I turn back and take another swing at the bag.

David walks around the bag and sits in the chair to my left. "You don't have to talk. I just need you to listen." He sighs. "Please, James."

I nod. I'll indulge him for a moment, and I'll keep punching the bag, pretending it's his face. Fuck, I'd love to punch him in the nose.

"We never meant to hurt you. I never meant to hurt you. It just happened." He pauses, inhaling deeply. "That sounds lame, but it's true. You know I'm not one for excuses, and I don't even have one. There is no excuse. There's only the truth."

I stop punching the bag and take a step to my right to see him better. I tilt my head, waiting for him to continue.

"I promise you, I never touched her until that night. I would never do that. She was eighteen before anything happened. I swear, man."

"Fine, but why my daughter? Why her?"

"She's captivated me. I can't even tell you how. It took me by surprise. I never thought I'd fall for her. I never meant to."

"Oh, you never meant to? How thoughtful." I take a threatening step toward him.

"I love her." He runs a hand through his hair and sighs, and with that nuclear declaration, he walks out.

A scream erupts from my lips. "Fuck!" I punch the bag with all my strength, watching everything fade behind me.

I'm not sure how much time has passed since he left, but before I know it, I've managed to sprain my wrist. Jessica comes into the garage and sees me wrapping it.

"I know you don't want to hear it, but you truly need to listen."

"Out with it," I huff.

"Skylar will always be your little girl, but she's matured now. She's not so little anymore. She's grown up. And, as much as we don't want to believe it, she is capable of making her own decisions. I've talked to her, and I've seen the way she looks at him. I've seen that look many times. She loves him."

"Right. She's eighteen. What the hell does she know about love?" My fists are clenched by my side.

"You. She knows you. She knows everything we've taught her. You've set a great example for her about what kind of relationship she should want to be in. We have set that example for her. We've raised her right, and she knows what's right and what's not. I have faith in her. You should too."

"What if I can't?"

"You need to, James. She deserves her chance at happiness. We can't tell her who she can and cannot love." Jessica stands up and walks over to me. "Let her be happy and make her own decisions. If it fails, then you can kill him."

If Jessica's right, and that's a big *if*, then it's either me or him.

Chapter Fifteen

Jessica

OH, MY HEART.

How she looks at him almost makes me wish I were young again.

James and I still look at each other that way, even to this day, many years later.

My baby girl is in love. A deep, honest, grown-up love. Not the puppy-dog love like most teenagers, but the type of love that's reserved for *the* love of your life.

While I'm not happy with how the whole thing went down, I can't say I'm surprised. From the moment they met, she's looked at David as though he's her world. She'd go through heaven and hell for this man. Love like that is rare, and Sky loves fiercely, like there's no tomorrow.

I knew her side of the story before I spoke to David. He'd never hurt her—not in a million years. Sky claims she started everything: the flirtations, coming on to him, wanting him, and more. I know she's not saying it to avoid getting him in trouble. The way her eyes light up when he walks into a room is something I've noticed for quite some time now. I don't blame her; he is easy on the eyes. Now that I know, it's easy to understand why she never had boyfriends—crushes, sure, but never dates she'd bring around the house, even after David moved out.

She let a boy take her to prom her senior year of high school, but he was a friend and nothing more. He knew it, too, and never tried to make any moves on her, from what I gathered. Olivia, her best friend, was good at fending those boys off.

My daughter has only ever had eyes for David, my husband's best friend.

Contrary to what my husband thinks, David didn't groom her or force her into doing anything she didn't want to. I feel it in my bones.

David says as much, too. When he finally told me the real reason why he moved out, I was speechless. He puts on a good face; I guess he's had to perfect it over the years. I'm grateful he moved out when he did, because honestly, I'm not sure what James would've done if he had found out about it then.

All the pieces fall into place as to why things changed how they did. They stopped running together in the early mornings. He stopped lingering around after dinner. He'd still debate and have long conversations with her at the table but would try not to get her all riled up. It didn't happen all at once, just small things over time. When he moved out, I knew it broke her heart. In my wildest dreams, I never would've imagined it was because she came on to him and he didn't want anything to happen between them.

The age gap between them is concerning, but I know from experience the heart wants what it wants. James has always told me that, just like he told Sky the same thing.

Her heart wants David, and no one can tell her otherwise. Who am I to stand in their way? He genuinely loves her with all his heart. I can see it. His eyes sparkled when he told me about it. I thought I'd feel sick knowing he had been under our roof for many years, but I didn't.

After what Kristie put him through, he bounced back and started having the time of his life. David deserves someone who will love and cherish him as Sky will. I want both of them to be happy.

Now, if only I can convince my husband to get over himself... That's going to take time. A lot of time.

Chapter Sixteen

David

TWO YEARS LATER...

Fuck, I love the way she squirms when I touch her. Bug quickly ends the phone call with her dad and yells my name, finally screaming her release. I've been teasing her for the past fifteen minutes, lazily pumping my fingers in and out of her sweet pussy.

She's dripping wet for me. I reward her frustration with an orgasm with my tongue before asking about the call.

"They're not coming here, right?" I ask, trailing my fingers up and down her stomach.

Bug snuggles against my shoulder and looks up at me. "You didn't have plans, did you?" A playful smile tugs at her lips.

"My *only* plan is to make you come over and over again. You've been a naughty girl this year, but instead of coal, I'll reward you until you can't stand."

"Well, that's going to have to wait. We're going to my parents' for dinner."

I groan. "And I guess James isn't too happy?"

"Of course not. But if he wants me there, you're coming too. He knows we're a package deal, no matter how much he doesn't like it." She rolls on top of me and grinds her hips. "Now, enough about my dad. It's Christmas Eve. Kiss me, David. Own me."

Christmas dinner this year comes with a side of hostility. Jessica is as friendly as always, wearing a larger-than-life smile as she hands out hot apple cider and snickerdoodle cookies—one of my favorite food combinations.

James hugs and greets Sky. When I stick out my hand, he glares at me.

We're off to a great start.

Jessica yells at him from the kitchen, and it makes me smile. Some things never change.

Bug turns to apologize to me on behalf of James.

"Don't you dare apologize to me. This isn't your fault. Apologize one more time, and you'll be punished."

"Spankings?" She fake pouts, but I see the fire blazing in her eyes.

"Twenty, and you can count on it," I whisper, but quickly pull away when James clears his throat behind me.

We make our way into the dining room and settle in for dinner. Bug gives me grief about hogging all the bread, like always. She'll never let me live it down: the first night I moved in, when Jessica made her famous lasagna with Texas toast. I snagged three pieces, and Bug scolded me because they're her favorite. Now, I always make sure to save her the last piece.

Jessica attempts to keep the small talk flowing, and after I compliment her on how great dinner is, James's ugly head roars to life.

"He betrayed us. In our own home, the one we welcomed him into with no strings attached. And to thank us, he sleeps with our daughter?"

"Dad!" Bug scowls. "I started this. I seduced him; I went after him. I did this, not him."

"You're a child. You don't know what you want," he spits out. "He's the adult. Adults should know better than to prey on children." He shoots me a look of disgust.

I would stay out of this, but he crossed a line. He does not get to talk to my Bug that way.

"That's enough, James." I raise my voice. "Hate me if you want, but you do not talk to Sky that way. She doesn't deserve your disgust or your comments. Out of respect for you, I did everything I could to ignore the pull between us and push her away. I avoided it as much as I could—even stopped coming around here until I couldn't anymore. Everything between us has been consensual..." I can't bring myself to say the rest. I'm horrified he even thinks I would do that.

We resume our dinner, the small talk finished. James reluctantly helps Jessica clear the table. I lean in for a quick kiss, then pull away too quickly. Bug starts apologizing, but I squeeze her thigh, hard, causing her to squirm and growl my name.

"That's twenty. Say sorry again and it'll be thirty," I warn.

Jessica comes in carrying a cheesecake with copious amounts of toppings. We eat the homemade cheesecake without conversation. Bug tenses every so often when James glares at me.

It's finally time to go, and we're getting our coats on when Bug accidentally steps on my foot. She apologizes before quickly covering her mouth.

My eyes light up like lights on a Christmas tree. *Oh, she's in for it. That's thirty.*

We say our goodbyes and walk down the driveway back to our car. The moment the front door closes, I grip Bug's wrist and pull her toward me.

"Two things will happen when we get home. One: you will grab the paddle. And two: you will wait for me bent over the back of the couch wearing only a bra, underwear, and your red heels. Understood?"

She nods. "Yes, sir."

"Good girl," I breathe, placing a hungry kiss on her lips.

Of all the times I've seen Bug bent over the couch, this one is the hottest. I take a moment to admire her ass. Those red high heels get me every time. Her toned legs look longer and drive me insane. Her tits hang over the back of the couch, her lacy red bra barely covering her nipples, and her matching thong draws my attention to her ass again.

Her breath is ragged, waiting. "Mm-hmm, you did such a good job," I mumble, tracing a finger down her side.

I grab a fistful of ass, squeeze, and then let go. The way her ass jiggles and sticks out just for me is almost enough to make me come. I swat her other cheek with my hand and watch it bounce.

"Ready?"

"Yes, si—" *Smack!*

"That's one. Count them."

"One," she whispers.

Smack!

"Two." I rub her now reddened skin before doing it again.

Smack, smack, smack.

"Three, four, five," she moans.

"I can't hear you," I tease her. *Smack!*

"Six!" she screams.

After rubbing both cheeks, I kick her legs further apart and touch my favorite part of her. "Soaking wet already." Her pussy pulses around my fingers. I withdraw my fingers and spank her again. And again. And again. I palm her cheeks, caressing the red-hot spots.

Each spank rewards me with her breathy count. Her pants come out as moans with each hit. My cock strains against my pants, begging to be freed. I *love* spanking her, maybe even more than she enjoys it.

I alternate between smacking her ass to see it bounce and pushing my fingers inside her. After twenty spankings, she's ready to go, juices dripping down her legs.

"Just a couple more, baby girl." The paddle comes down on her ass eight more times.

"Twenty-eight," she pants.

There are two left, and she needs those last two. But instead, I free my cock and quickly sink deep inside her.

She gasps and shudders beneath me. "Yesss..."

I move her hair to the side and kiss her neck. "I couldn't wait any longer to be inside you. I. Need. You." I thrust into her hard and unyielding, frenzied. "Such a naughty fucking girl."

"Oh, fuck," she cries out. "Can I come, please?"

What a good girl . . .

"Since you asked nicely." I grin and slow my thrusts. It's torturous for both of us. My cock slides out of her until only the head is left.

"No," she whimpers. "Don't stop."

I slam back into her, then repeat the movements. Her entire body shakes on the third one. "Come for me, Bug."

She holds on one more time and then ultimately falls apart, screaming my name. My Bug is so beautiful when she comes. My cock twitches and empties into her pussy. Her name falls from my lips as I come. *Skylar.*

After a moment, I slide out of her, carry her to the couch, and rid her of her clothes and shoes. She looks at me through her lashes and says, "This will never get old."

Never.

Chapter Seventeen

David

Present day...

I've never seen this much pain on Bug's face before. Not even when we've gone a little too far pushing her limits during playtime.

One nurse is trying to take her vitals, while another walks around the small room getting things ready.

"Bug." I rush to her side and place my hand on top of hers. Her knuckles are white from gripping the bed railing so hard.

"Here comes the next one. Remember to breathe," the nurse says.

Instead of a breath, Bug lets out a gargled scream.

I pull some damp hair away from her face and tuck it behind her ear. "You're doing so good, baby girl."

"Don't say that! That's what got us here in the first place!"

Both nurses hide their smiles and try not to laugh.

"Okay, you're doing bad?" I try.

"Ugh!" She growls at me.

One of the nurses sits on the stool and rolls between Bug's legs, then ducks her head under the sheet. "Let's see how far along you are."

"Nine months?" I guess, earning a chuckle from the other nurse. Bug shoots me a glare and huffs.

"No, centimeters. She needs to be at a ten before we can start pushing. She's at a six right now." The nurse removes the gloves and throws them in the trash can to her right. "And honey, you're sure you don't want an epidural?"

Bug nods. It's in her birthing plan. She doesn't want any drugs unless medically necessary.

Over the next few minutes, another couple of contractions run through her body. We practice breathing together. She squeezes my hand with each one that rips through her. After half an hour, one of the nurses rechecks her and tells us it's almost time.

The doctor comes in and greets us. "I hear it's time for us to have a baby. Are you ready, Mom?"

She nods frantically. "Please get her out."

"Dad, here's what you'll do. You'll hold her leg up and push her knee to her chest when she pushes. Nurse Susan will do the same to her other leg. Got it?"

"Yes, ma'am." I step closer to the bed, getting into position.

"Alright, Mom. Another one is coming. This time I want you to push with everything you've got. Three . . . two . . . one, push!"

Nurse Susan and I hold Bug's legs up as she bears down and pushes.

"And rest. You're doing great." The doctor looks up at Bug. "You doing okay?"

She groans, not answering.

"You're almost there, baby girl. Keep it up." I kiss her forehead.

We cycle through the contractions, each one lasting a little longer.

"Next one is the big one . . . In three . . . two . . . one, push!"

Bug screams as she pushes. I take a peek, even though I told her I wouldn't. What a fucking sight. My baby is almost out. One more and . . . there she is. Our daughter.

The nurse motions toward the baby. "Dad, are you doing the honors?"

My eyes widen. I forgot about this part. I set Bug's leg down, walk around to the doctor's left side, and take a pair of scissors from the second nurse. The doctor points between the two clamps, and I cut the cord.

The baby immediately cries, and the second nurse whisks her away to a small table to the left.

"David?" Bug calls for me.

"I'm right here, baby girl." I rush back to her side and brush the hair out of her face. "You did it."

"We did it." She sighs, smiling.

A moment later, our baby girl lies nestled between Bug's breasts, skin to skin.

"Oh, Bug. She's beautiful."

She smiles at me with the most adorable smile. "She's everything."

My two girls are the most beautiful creatures on the planet.

Nurse Susan comes over and asks if we need anything. I assure her we don't, but she tells us to press the call button if we do. She'll come back later.

I kiss Bug on the forehead before heading out of the room to call Jessica. Bug didn't want them at the hospital because she didn't want James to cause a scene. Jessica was disappointed but understood. We've been together for almost seven years, and James still has a chip on his shoulder. Jessica and I talk for a few minutes and arrange a time for them to stop by tomorrow. I'd make myself scarce, allowing them some alone time with their granddaughter.

When I walk back into the room a few minutes later, Bug is asleep with our little girl on her chest. Our little one cries the smallest of cries, and without waking Bug, I grab our girl and cradle her in my arms.

We sit in the rocking chair Nurse Susan brought in. My baby girl sleeps soundly in my arms. Her puffy eyes conceal their color, but I know she'll have Bug's hazel eyes, just like she has my ears and nose.

Our little girl.

Bayleigh Rae Sullivan.

Seven pounds, four ounces. Twenty-one inches long.

My little baby girl.

She opens her eyes, and my heart melts. Yep, she has her mother's eyes. With just one look, she has me wrapped around her tiny fingers. Love at first sight. I'll go to the ends of the earth for her.

"Hi, Bayleigh," I coo at her. "I'm your daddy."

Bug's voice drifts toward me. "You look perfect."

I smile at Bayleigh, then look at Bug. "And you're awake. You should be sleeping."

"As if. The picture alone is enough to keep me awake for a lifetime." She beams at me from the bed.

There's a small knock at the door before Nurse Susan enters. "You ready to try breastfeeding?"

I place our baby back into her mother's arms and retake my seat. The nurse helps position Bayleigh and talks through the steps with Bug, how to hold her straight with both the baby's head and body facing toward the nipple. Bayleigh latches on for a moment before pulling away.

"It might take some time. Some take to it right away; others don't. Give her another moment, then offer it to her again."

Bug nods, glancing at me with hopeful eyes. I stand up, walk to her side, and whisper something crude in her ear. She gasps. "Go away."

Nurse Susan chuckles as she helps Bug get Bayleigh positioned again. Bayleigh turns her head.

"It's okay, sweet baby. Go ahead." Bug offers her nipple again. This time Bayleigh latches on and sucks. Bug flinches slightly.

"It might be uncomfortable, but the discomfort should ease as you both get the hang of it. When her sucking becomes long and slow, or if it looks like she's falling asleep, you can break the suction. Burp her and wait a few minutes, then you can try the other breast. It's okay if she doesn't take to that one; she might not be hungry. Next time, you'll start with that one, and we'll go from there." Nurse Susan takes Bayleigh's vitals while in Bug's arms. "Everything sounds great. I'll come check on you guys in a little bit."

Bug lays her head back onto the bed and watches Bayleigh. I take a quick picture of them lying together. I've already taken a couple of pictures—I want to remember everything about today. She might kill me later, but it'll be worth it. There's nothing else in this world I'd rather look at. She's a canvas where our connection has painted a vivid tapestry of shared laughter and memorable moments.

A fierce, overwhelming tug pulls at my heart. Even though Bayleigh is only a couple of hours old, I already want to protect her from everything. Come hell or high water, I'll always protect her.

Oh, man. I *really* fucked up.

The weight of how James has felt this whole time hits me like a ton of bricks. I won't apologize for falling in love with his daughter. Never. It wasn't a mistake. But I can apologize for the way he found out.

I need to set this right.

Not just for Bug, but for my Bayleigh too.

Chapter Eighteen

James

Three years later...

Grandfather. Grandpa. Gramps. Pop. Paw Paw.

She can call me whatever she wants, my sweet granddaughter. I see so much of Sky in her. She's got my daughter's eyes and smile, and cute little dimples that are to die for.

She's got David's nose, ears, and hair—a full head of hair, too. As much as I strongly dislike him, I can't help but be happy when my granddaughter is around. I know she's a part of him, but nothing else matters when we're together.

Jessica *loves* to babysit. I'll change diapers, protesting the whole way, but when it's just me and Bayleigh, my demeanor crumbles. I'm a big old softie. It's hard to say no when I see her mother's eyes looking at me.

I could never say no to Sky, either. That's how we're in the predicament we're in currently.

They've been a couple for nine years now. That's how old my baby girl was when they met—nine years old. I've known for eight of the past nine years that nothing nefarious happened under my roof. David didn't physically or mentally hurt my baby girl.

I did.

My actions were atrocious. I couldn't stop it. All I saw was red, in the worst ways.

Sure, I'm still angry and hurt over how I found out about them. Granted, I might have acted the same way if they told me at a different time, so we'll never really know.

In the past nine years, David's done exactly what I expressed I wanted. He's stayed away, only coming around when necessary. If they both come to the house, I make myself scarce. If Sky comes over, I'll come out of my hiding spot. I miss my baby girl.

I'm polite when I see him, even at work. Our interactions are minimal, and everyone knows not to call us into the same meeting. How we've lasted this long working together, I'll never know. Thankfully, I'm not yelling or cursing at him anymore. I thought a lot about firing his ass, but he's too brilliant to lose. I'd never forgive myself if I let him go. Neither would my wife or daughter.

It's taken me a long time to get here, which is why when he asked to see me, I agreed.

I know what he wants.

It's about fucking time, too.

"Two, please," a voice next to me says. The bartender nods, pulls out two beers, and pops the tops, then slides one in front of me and the other in front of him.

My former best friend.

"David." I spin on my stool and face him.

"James. Thanks for meeting with me."

"How's Bayleigh?"

"Oh, she's great! Finally wrote her name today. Made Sky's day. She's been working so hard with her." David sips his beer.

"That's fantastic. And how's Sky?" My relationship with my daughter is still rocky, but it's slowly improving.

"She's good. Feeling extra tired lately—Bayleigh has been running her a little ragged. Did she tell Jessica about Bayleigh entering the threenager stage? Damn girl wants to do everything by herself, damn the consequences."

"Yeah, that sounds like Sky at that age. She'll grow out of it." I down the last of my beer.

"Oh, she's feisty, alright. Both of them." He laughs. "The reason I asked you here, actually, is for both of them."

"Oh?"

"I cherish them both and am eternally grateful they're in my life. Sky brings out the best in me, and my love for her is unmatched. I plan on spending the rest of my life making your daughter and granddaughter feel loved, happy, and respected. They're my family, and I want to make it official. With your blessing, I'd like to ask Sky to marry me."

I blow out a quick breath but let him sit there for a moment before smiling widely. "Well, it's about damn time you asked!" I pull him into a hug. "You're still an idiot, but welcome back to the family, man."

David's face fills with relief like he can't believe I've given my blessing. When he asked to meet privately, I immediately knew what he wanted. For a split second, I thought about saying no, but all I've ever wanted is for my daughter to be happy and loved as she should be. If she's happy with my best friend and he's who her heart wants, then it's about time I step out of the goddamn way.

Chapter Nineteen

Sky

THE VIBRANT FOLIAGE DRIFTS around us as David and I stroll through the plaza park. The air is crisp and serene, carrying the sweet scent of fallen leaves. It's giving sweater-weather vibes. Give me a hot apple cider and it'd be perfect.

David's unusually quiet. Lately, he's been going on about his latest project at work and bouncing ideas off me. Today, he doesn't speak as he intertwines his fingers in mine. The quiet doesn't bother me—having a toddler wears me out most days. I'll take the quiet any time.

We reach the fountain in the middle of the plaza, and David pauses. He gently tugs on my hand and steers me toward a beautifully decorated picnic blanket to the right. While not many people are out today, there's no mistaking it's meant for us.

My eyes widen as I take in the scene before me. Along with the red-and-white checkered blanket, there's an assortment of flowers, a bottle of champagne and two glasses, something in a white box, and a small boombox in the corner. A soft melody plays from the speakers, adding an extra touch of calm.

David helps me sit on the blanket, carefully avoiding spilling anything in the grass. Once settled in, he glances around before getting up on one knee.

My breath hitches, and I wait, eyes wide.

"Bug, from the moment we met, you brought immeasurable joy and love into my life. Never in my wildest dreams did I think meeting you would turn me upside down in the best way possible. You've shown me the meaning of unconditional love and have cheered me on through some of the most difficult times. Today, surrounded by the beauty of nature and the knowledge that anything is possible, I want to ask you the most important I could ever imagine." His voice is warm and fills my heart. The butterflies spring to life, and I nod, encouraging him to continue. "Skylar Julie Wyatt, my Bug, will you make me the happiest man in the world and marry me?"

Tears spring to my eyes as I nod enthusiastically, unable to find my voice. Amidst the overwhelming emotions, I extend my hand toward him. David carefully slips an intense blue round-cut diamond engagement ring onto my finger.

The ring glistens in the sunlight, and I take a moment to admire David's great taste before pouncing on him, knocking him back into the grass. He laughs that thunderous laugh that always warms my heart.

"Yes," I mutter in between kisses. "A thousand times yes."

We kiss until I remember we're in public at the park. *Oops.* I climb off him and sit back on the blanket, smoothing it out around me. I hold out my hand, palm down, and admire the ring, my thoughts drifting away with the wind.

Everything about this is perfect. The park, the person, the significance of the moment—a moment that marks the beginning of a new chapter for our entwined souls. Time stands still as David wraps his arms around me, and my heart feels like it'll burst, overflowing with joy and happiness.

Surrounded by the whispers of nature and the promise of a lifetime of shared adventures, we celebrate our engagement. David pops the cork off the bottle and pours me some champagne. A little bit is fine . . . I smirk as he hands me the glass and clinks it against his.

The sun sets behind us as we finish the cookies from Sweet Apples Bakery. I'm not ready to leave this moment, so I pull David a little bit closer and rest my head on his shoulder.

"You make me the happiest woman alive, David." I tilt my head up and plant a soft kiss on his cheek.

"And you make me the happiest man in the whole world, Bug." We sit there for a few more minutes before David sighs. "We better go rescue your mother from Bayleigh. She's probably pulling her hair out by now."

I groan. Bayleigh is going through her threenager phase. We barely made it through the terrible twos, and now she's a threenager who knows *everything*.

"What'd you promise her? There's no way she'd voluntarily watch Bayleigh right now."

"Nothing. She was happy to do it." He shrugs. My skepticism must be apparent, because he says, "I swear!"

"You're lucky she likes you." I wag my finger at him playfully.

We clean up the area, leaving it better than we found it, and take our time walking back to the car.

The doorbell rings, and I mentally kick myself for forgetting to put the sign up. Bayleigh absolutely *hates* the doorbell.

I'm not sure I can top David's proposal, but here goes nothing. "David, grab the door!" I shout from the kitchen.

Just as I put the finishing touches on Bayleigh's outfit, he walks into the kitchen and sets the pizzas on the island. "Bug, why'd you order three pizzas? Plan on having company?"

"Not that I'm aware of," I say nonchalantly, moving around the kitchen with Bayleigh's back to him.

He opens the first pizza box, ready to grab a slice, but stops and chuckles, looking at me. "Are either of the other two pizzas actual pizzas? Or did you just order three cookie pizzas?" He slides the top box to the side. The cookie pizza is decorated with two colors of frosting—not that he noticed.

"You'll have to wait and see." I wink and finish putting Bayleigh in the high chair.

I turn around just in time to see him lift the lid of the second box. The look of confusion on his face almost gives me away. This box has the tiny brownie bites.

"How many times do I have to remind you you can't just eat dessert for dinner?" he jests playfully.

"Hardy har har," I say with a laugh. "Open the next one. I'm hungry."

As if on cue, Bayleigh picks up her fork and hits it against the tray. "Daddy, food please," she says.

His eyes light up like Christmas lights every time she calls him daddy. It never gets old seeing the look on his face, the look of pure admiration and love he has for her, our baby girl.

He turns to give her a quick wave. "One second, baby girl."

I smile, unable to hold back the laughter any longer.

"What's so funny?" He gives me a side-eye glance.

"Nothing," I say. "Yet." I wave my hand toward the pizza box.

He moves the second one to the side and slowly opens the third box.

"It's a pizza," he says flatly. Then he fully opens the box and takes a step back. "Wait . . . are you serious?" His eyes meet mine, daring me to be wrong.

"I'm sure." When I ordered the pizza, I asked Milo to make it in the shape of a heart and spell out "Baby 2" in pepperoni. He closes the distance between us and sweeps me off the ground, then spins me in a circle. "Oof!" I say, then squeal.

"I'm going to be a daddy! Again!" His laugh rings deep in my bones, and he gives me a panty-melting kiss.

"Daddy!" Bayleigh shouts.

He sets me down, walks over to his little girl in the high chair, and kisses her forehead. She's smiling and giggling when he pulls away.

"Daddy!" She blows him a kiss. Such a sweetheart when she's not a hurricane tearing through my living room.

David gives her a puzzled look and cocks his head to the side. "BayBay, do you know what your shirt says?"

She shakes her head.

"Your momma didn't tell you? Shame on her . . ." He gives me a pouty look, then turns back to Bayleigh. "It says 'Big Sister.' Do you know what that means?"

She shakes her head again. "Daddy, I'm hungry."

He kisses her forehead again and smooths down her hair. "It means you'll have a brother or sister soon."

"Daddy, food now!" She hits the fork against the tray again.

I roll my eyes, and David laughs. He laughs as though it's the first time she's done it; as if she hasn't done it every meal three times a day for the past two weeks.

"Anything for my BayBay."

Epilogue

Sky

EIGHTEEN MONTHS LATER...

Olivia's pacing is driving me up the wall, even more so than it usually does. "Dammit, woman, can you stop pacing?"

"I have to be worried enough for the both of us!" she shrieks.

"Jeez, it's not like you're the one getting married." I shake my head, pry Harper off my tit, then hand her to my mom.

The florist has yet to arrive at the venue, and while I'm not terribly worried about her being late, Olivia is all over the place. If my bouquet doesn't arrive in time, that's totally fine.

No one tells you how hard it is to plan a wedding *and* plan for the arrival of your second child before your first is in kindergarten. It's been a long year and then some, but today is finally coming together.

The sun beams through the window, bathing the bridal suite in a warm glow. Outside, the wedding planner, Avery, is busy pointing people to where they're needed. We're getting married in a gorgeous garden just outside of Crimson. All the trees are in full bloom, giving a backdrop of vibrant flowers in different hues. Outside of the bridal flowers, petals for Bayleigh, the groomsmen's boutonnieres, and decorating the arch, the greenery is taken care of.

None of that prevents me from marrying the man of my dreams. I couldn't care less if I got married without flowers. All I need are my girls and my man.

Avery did a spectacular job working with the florist, trailing delicate roses entwined with baby's breath over the gold-wrapped arch. Thankfully, the arch arrived the day before, otherwise I'd be a little more concerned.

Dozens of chairs line both sides of the aisles behind a big chalkboard sign that indicates no one is picking sides. We're all family; sit where you please. In a small town like Crimson, making people pick sides would be a crime.

"Finally!" Olivia gasps and rushes over to the florist, grabbing the boutonnieres on her way out the door.

"Pay her no mind," Mom tells the florist, who hands the bridal bouquet and the rest of the flowers to her.

"I'm so sorry for being late! I got a flat tire and had to wait for someone to change it. I'm old, you know." She laughs at her joke. Millie isn't old by any standards. She's in her early forties, with a passion for turning a simple flower into a thing of beauty.

My mom waves her hand. "Neither of us was worried. We knew you'd make it." She rips off the check she just signed and hands it to Millie. "Thank you."

"Good luck, girly!" Millie waves in my direction and leaves as quickly as she came.

"You ready, Sky?"

I sneak another glance outside and realize people are starting to fill the chairs, then turn to look at my mom. She's stunning in her pale-pink bridesmaid dress. "Almost." I walk over to the mirror and take another good look at myself. My lips turn into a smile, and my heart feels so full. "Okay. I'm ready."

My mom hands me my bouquet and fusses with my veil.

Knock, knock.

The door opens a tiny bit, and Avery sticks her head in. "Five-minute warning. We're all set out here, even Bayleigh. She won't stop bouncing; she's so excited."

"Of course she is." That's my Bayleigh—too much excitement for one little body.

A warm melody floats down the hallway. "And that's my queue. Jessica, get ready." Avery nods to my mom and then closes the door.

My mom turns to me with tears lining her eyes. "Honey, you look beautiful. David is a very lucky man."

The dress hugs my curvy figure and bellows out at the bottom. An ivory lace gown was the perfect pick. Its strapless sweetheart neckline gives me cleavage for days, while the beads shimmer in the light.

"Don't cry on me now. I can't smudge my mascara." I fan my face to help dry the tears.

She laughs. "You and me both!" She opens the door for me and peeks out. "It's time."

I reach for her hand, and she squeezes it. We walk to the entrance of the garden, and I gasp. The first thing I notice is David standing at the altar, waiting for me. He's dressed in a tailored navy-blue suit with a crisp white shirt and a pale-pink tie. His eyes sparkle with excitement and laughter as he watches our daughter skip down the aisle. His soul and my soul are one with her. We became one long before we say "I do."

There she is, the girl of the hour, doing the most important job there is. Styled with playful pigtails and a pale-pink dress of her own, she skips barefoot down the aisle. With each skip she takes, she tosses a handful of petals in the air and squeals as they fall on her and onto the ground around her. Right before she gets to the altar where the babysitter awaits, she turns around and shouts, "I did it, Mommy!"

Laughter sounds out across the garden, and all the heads turn toward me. I wave my hand toward Olivia, who should've already been walking down the aisle. Elliott takes her arm and gently tugs, signaling it's their turn. "Oops," she mouths to me.

I grin and shake my head, then turn to look for my dad. He's supposed to walk me down the aisle. *If he shows up.* "Where's Dad?" I whisper to my left.

Instead of answering me, she starts her saunter down the aisle to my awaiting groom.

"Is the offer still open?"

Relief washes over me when I recognize his voice. "Yes, please."

"Anything for my Sky." My dad steps out from behind me and holds his arm out for me to grasp. "You ready?"

"Yes." I take a deep breath. "I'm ready."

"Okay." He leans over and kisses my cheek. "Let's go."

Elvis Presley's voice rings out, and my dad takes the first step toward the altar. We walk in sync down the aisle toward my future husband, toward my dad's best friend.

We're almost there when I look up, and my breath catches in my throat. The way David looks at me, with pure lust and admiration, sends my heart fluttering. Once we reach the altar, David reaches out to grab my hand, but before he can, my dad leans closer and whispers something in his ear. I can't hear him, but whatever he says causes David to chuckle.

"I love you, my baby girl." My dad kisses my cheek once more before placing my hand in David's.

We turn to face each other as the officiant begins the ceremony. Our vows echo through the garden—promises of unconditional love, dreams, and devotion. The emotion behind our words is undeniable. Next, we exchange rings, and I slide the band onto David's ring finger. He does the same with mine and then the officiant pronounces us husband and wife. Our wedding is a testament to the power of love, friendship, and commitment, and how the three intertwine without a moment's notice.

Everyone cheers when David's hand cups my cheek and he draws me in for a kiss. A tug on my dress breaks us apart.

"Mommy, I have to pee."

The babysitter comes running after Bayleigh, muttering her apologies, and grabs Bayleigh's hand, pulling her away.

"Ever the cockblocker," David says for my ears only.

Oh, the plans I have for this man. I smirk at him and wink. "Just you wait."

The End

Thanks for reading She Calls Me Daddy! Did you enjoy reading the second part of David and Bug's story? Please consider leaving a review on Amazon and Goodreads!

Quote

Lucy: Oh, gee, Ethel, thanks. It's times like these when you know what friends are for.
Ethel: If I'd known this was what friends were for, I'd have signed up as an enemy!

I Love Lucy - Season 6 Episode 23

She Calls Me Daddy Playlist

The World by Brad Paisley
Bad Boys by Inner Circle
Dear Agony by Breaking Benjamin
Punching Bag by Set It Off
Red Dress by Sophia Scott
Shackles by Steven Rodriguez
Lips of a Witch by Austin Giorgio
Ain't No Mountain High Enough by Marvin Gaye and Tammi Terrell
Can't Help Falling in Love by Elvis Presley
Butterfly Kisses by Bob Carlisle
Bad Word by Panicland

Sky and David's Recipe

Snickerdoodle Cookies

Cookie:
1 cup butter, softened to room temperature
1 ⅓ cups sugar
1 egg
2 tsp vanilla extract
3 cups flour
2 tsp cream of tartar*
2 ½ tsp cinnamon

Topping:
¼ cup sugar
1 tsp cinnamon

1. Preheat the oven to 375°F.

2. In a small bowl, mix together the sugar and cinnamon for the topping. Set aside.

3. In a mixing bowl, cream the butter until smooth. Then add in the sugar. Mix until light and fluffy.

4. Add in the egg and vanilla extract. Mix until combined.

5. Add in the rest of the dry ingredients, but slowly add the flour, and mix thoroughly.

6. Scoop into little balls** and roll the dough into the topping mixture.

7. Put the cookies onto a tray and bake for 10-11 minutes. DO NOT OVERBAKE.

8. Let them cool on the tray, then transfer to a cooling rack or airtight container.

Notes:
*Cream of tartar is what makes the cookie. It's a *must*.
**A cookie scoop is preferred but you can use whatever is on hand.

Acknowledgments

Tiffany: thanks for helping me with names. You broke the tie and then some. Love you, bestie!

Chris: as always, thank you for listening to me endlessly vent about the book. You're the best trooper ever.

Gwen: continue to use that whip, please! It makes me write the words.

Rachelle: thank you for another amazing round of edits! Your feedback keeps me going, and I *might* know when to use a comma or a period for dialogue tags.

Dee: your eagle eye for last moment touches makes this ever so special.

Jillian: the cover is gorgeous! Thank you for the time you've spent on both covers for David and Sky.

Read more from Zoey Zane

Out Now

a beautiful broken life
He Calls Me Bug
(previously in Cheaters: A Dark Romance Anthology)
Countdown Madness
Naughty Doctor
Unwrapping Spring Break
She Calls Me Daddy

Coming Soon

Naughty Stalker
Naughty Planner
Sweet Like Sugar, Thick Like Honey

Meet Zoey

Zoey Zane is an author and poet, but will always be a zealous reader at heart. She has a love for dark romance and thrillers, the two genres that dominate most of the space on her bookshelves. Zoey lives in Tennessee with her husband, their son, and their two adorable pit bulls.

ZOEY ZANE

You can find me at zoeyzane.net, by scanning the QR code, or on the sites below!

- amazon.com/Zoey-Zane/e/B08K56BJZ2/
- facebook.com/zoeyzaneauthor
- bookbub.com/authors/zoey-zane
- goodreads.com/author/show/20671544.Zoey_Zane
- instagram.com/justmekendra/

Made in the USA
Columbia, SC
06 August 2024